THE CAROUSEL

"DELIGHTFUL . . . It exudes comfort as it entertains."

—*Publishers Weekly*

"ENORMOUS CHARM AND WARMTH!"
—*Kirkus Reviews*

"A romantic tale imbued with several comforting lessons on loving, friendship, and family ties."
—*Booklist*

"Enjoyable and satisfying."
—*Chattanooga News-Free Press*

"A romance with some mystery and considerable depth to commend it."
—*Tulsa World*

"[An] agreeable compound of beautiful scenery and warm and loving relationships."
—*Library Journal*

"A tender story of age, and youth, friendship and love . . . LOVELY!"
—*Romantic Times*

THE CAROUSEL

ROSAMUNDE PILCHER

St. Martin's Paperbacks

THE CAROUSEL

Copyright © 1982 by Rosamunde Pilcher.

Cover photograph © Foodpix.

All rights reserved. No part of this book may be used or reproduced in any manner whatsoever without written permission except in the case of brief quotations embodied in critical articles or reviews. For information address St. Martin's Press, 175 Fifth Avenue, New York, NY 10010.

Library of Congress Catalog Card Number: 82-5629

ISBN: 0-312-92629-4
EAN: 80312-92629-8

Printed in the United States of America

St. Martin's Press hardcover edition published 1985
St. Martin's Paperbacks edition / December 1986

St. Martin's Paperbacks are published by St. Martin's Press, 175 Fifth Avenue, New York, NY 10010.

30 29 28 27 26 25 24 23 22 21

Chapter 1

My MOTHER STOOD in the middle of her pretty sitting room, filled with September sunshine, and said, "Prue, you must be going out of your mind."

She looked as though she were about to burst into tears of disappointment, but I knew that she would not, because tears would destroy her faultless maquillage, would make her face swell, turn down her mouth, and accentuate unbecoming lines. However exasperated, she would never cry. Her appearance mattered to her almost more than anything else, and now she stood across the hearth rug from me, immaculately turned out in a raspberry pink woollen suit and a white silk shirt, with her gold earrings and her charm bracelet, and pretty silvery hair crisp and curly.

She struggled, however, to contain a conflict of destructive emotions: anger, motherly concern, but mostly disappointment. I felt very sorry for her.

I said, "Oh, come on, Ma, it's not the end of the world." Even as I said it, it sounded pretty feeble, which it probably was.

"For the first time in your life, you seem to have got involved with a really suitable man . . ."

"Darling, 'suitable's a terribly old-fashioned word . . ."

"He's charming, he's steady, he's got a good job, and he comes from the right sort of family. You're twenty-three and it's time you settled down, got married and had children and a home of your own."

"Ma, he hasn't even *asked* me to marry him."

"Of course he hasn't. He wants to do it properly—take you home, introduce you to his mother. There's nothing wrong with that. And it's obvious the way his mind is running. You only have to see the two of you together to know that he's wildly in love with you."

"Nigel is incapable of being wildly anything."

"Honestly, Prue, I don't know what you're looking for."

"I'm not looking for anything."

We had had this conversation so often that I knew my part word for word, as though I had sat down and learned it by heart. "I've got everything I want. A job I like, a little flat of my own—"

"You can hardly call that one-room basement a flat—"

"And I don't feel like settling down."

"You're twenty-three. I was nineteen when I was married."

I nearly said, *and divorced six years later,* but I didn't. However maddened by her, you couldn't say things like that to my mother. I knew that she had a will of iron and an inner core of steel, which nearly always ensured that she got her own way, but there was something vulnerable about her— her delicate build, her enormous blue eyes, her rampant femininity—that precluded harsh words.

So I opened my mouth and then shut it again, and looked at her hopelessly. She gazed back at me, reproachful but not reproaching, and I understood for perhaps the thousandth time why my father, from the moment they set eyes on each other, had been lost. They had married because she was totally irresistible, and he was exactly what she had been searching for ever since she first realised that there was such a thing as an opposite sex.

My father is called Hugh Shackleton. In those days he worked in London, in a merchant bank in the City, with a life-style that was solid and a future that was bright. But he was basically a fish out of water. The Shackletons were a Northumberland family, and my father had been brought up there on a farm called Windyedge, where the pasture fields ran down to the cold North Sea and the winter gales blew straight in from the Ural Mountains. My father never lost his love of the country, or ceased to yearn for it. When he married my mother, the farm was being managed by his older brother, but about the time that I was five years old, this brother tragically was killed in a hunting accident. My father travelled to Northumberland for the funeral. He stayed away for five days, and by the time he returned to us, his mind was made up. He told my mother that he intended resigning from his job, selling the house in London, and returning to Windyedge.

He was going to be a farmer.

The rows and arguments, the tears and recriminations that followed this announcement are amongst the earliest of my truly unhappy memories. My mother tried everything to make him change his mind, but my father remained adamant. In the end she fired her final gun. If he returned to Northumberland, he would return alone. Rather to her surprise, he did this. Perhaps he thought that she would follow, but she could be just as stubborn. Within the year they were duly divorced. The house in Paulton Square was sold and my mother moved to another, smaller one, near Parson's Green. I, naturally, stayed with her, but I always went to Northumberland for a couple of weeks every year, just to keep in touch with my father. After a bit he married again; a shy, horsy girl whose tweed skirts were always slightly seated and whose clear and freckled face had never known so much as the touch of a powder puff. They were very happy. They are still very happy. And I am glad.

But for my mother it was not so easy. She had married my father because he seemed to conform to a pattern of masculinity that she could understand and admire. She never delved beneath the veneer of the pinstripe suit and the briefcase. She had no wish to uncover any hidden depths. But the Shackletons were full of surprises, and to my mother's horror, I inherited most of them. My dead uncle had not only been a farmer but an amateur musician of some achievement. My father in his spare time stitched the most beautiful tapestries. But it was their sister Phoebe who was the true rebel. An artist and an accomplished painter, she was a character of such originality, with such careless regard of day-to-day conventions, that my mother had a hard time coming to terms with her sister-in-law.

As a young woman Phoebe had based herself in London, but in her middle years she wiped the dust of the city from her shoes and went to live in Cornwall, where she cohabited happily with a charming man, a sculptor, called Chips Armitage. They never married—I think because his wife would not divorce him—and when he died he left his little Victorian Gothic house in Penmarron to Phoebe, and she had lived there ever since.

Despite this small social hiccup my mother could not completely write Phoebe off, because Phoebe was my godmother. Every now and then my mother and I would be invited to stay with her. The letters always made it perfectly clear that Phoebe would be happy to have me on my own. But my mother feared her bohemian influence, and on the principle that if she couldn't lick the Shackletons, she would join them, she always—at least when I was a child—accompanied me on these visits.

The first time we travelled to Cornwall, I was filled with anxiety. I was only a child, but I knew well that my mother and Phoebe had nothing in common, and I dreaded two weeks of disagreements and prickly silences. But I underestimated Phoebe's perception. She took care of the situation by introducing my mother to Mrs. Tolliver. Mrs. Tolliver lived in the White Lodge at Penmarron and had a perfectly conventional little circle of friends, who were charmed to include my pretty mother in their bridge afternoons and small dinner parties.

With them, she would contentedly play cards on the bright days while Phoebe and I walked on the beach, or set up our easels by the old seawall, or drove inland in the battered old Volkswagen that Phoebe used as a mobile studio, to climb the moor and lose ourselves in landscapes that lay drowned in a white and shimmering light that seemed reflected from the very sea itself.

Despite my mother's antagonism, Phoebe exerted enormous influences on my life. Unconscious influences, in the shape of my inherited talent for drawing. And other, more practical influences—pressures, maybe—which bolstered my determination to study in Florence, to go to art school, and which finally culminated in getting me my present job with the Marcus Bernstein Gallery in Cork Street.

And now it was because of Phoebe that we quarrelled. Nigel Gordon had come into my life some months ago. He was the first totally conventional person I had ever even mildly liked, and when I brought him home to meet my mother, she could not hide her delight. He was charming with her, flirting a little and bringing her flowers, and when she learned that he had invited me to Scotland to stay with his family and meet his mother, her excitement knew no bounds. She had already bought me a pair of tweed knickerbockers to wear "on the moor," and beyond this I knew that her imagination was in full flight to the final climax of engagement notices in the *Times*, engraved invitations, and a London wedding with me in a white creation designed to look well from the back.

But at the last moment, Phoebe had put an end to all these pretty fancies. She had, of all things, broken her arm, and the day she returned from hospital to Holly Cottage, her little house, with the arm rigid in a plaster cast, she telephoned to beg me to come and keep her company. It wasn't that she couldn't perfectly well look after herself, but she was not able to drive the car, and to remain immobilized until the cast came off was more than she could bear.

As I listened to her voice over the phone, I was filled with an extraordinary sense of relief, and it was only then that I admitted to myself that I didn't want to go north to stay with the Gordons. I was not ready to become so deeply involved with Nigel. Subconsciously I had been longing for some sound excuse to wriggle out of the arrangement. And here it was, presented to me on a plate. Without even hesitating, I told Phoebe that I would go. Then I told Nigel that I couldn't go to Scotland. And now I was telling my mother.

She was, predictably, devastated.

"Cornwall. With Phoebe." She made it sound like the worst sort of dead end.

"I must go, Ma." I tried to make her smile. "You know she's hopeless at driving that old car of hers, even with two arms."

But she was beyond amusement. "It's so rude, crying off at the last moment. You'll never be invited again. And what will Nigel's mother think?"

"I'll write to her. I'm sure she'll understand."

"And with Phoebe . . . you'll meet nobody with Phoebe except a lot of unwashed students and extraordinary women in hand-woven ponchos."

"Perhaps Mrs. Tolliver will come up with some suitable man for me."

"It's nothing to joke about."

I said, gently, "It is *my* life."

"You've always said that. You said it when you took yourself off to live in that gruesome basement in Islington. Islington, of all places."

"It's very trendy."

"And when you enrolled at that horrible art school . . ."

"At least I've got a perfectly respectable job. You must admit that."

"You ought to be married. And then you wouldn't have to have a job."

"Even if I were married, I wouldn't want to give it up."

"But, Prue, it's not a future. I want you to have a proper life."

"I think it is a proper life."

We eyed each other for a long moment. Then my mother sighed deeply, resigned and apparently mortally wounded. And I knew that for the time being, the argument was over.

She said, sounding pathetic, "I'll never understand you."

I went to give her a hug. "Don't try," I told her. "Just cheer up and go on liking me. I'll send you a postcard from Cornwall."

I had decided not to drive a car to Penmarron but to travel by train. The next morning I took a taxi to Paddington, found the right platform and the right coach. I had reserved a seat, but the train was not full; by the middle of September the flood of holidaymakers had ceased. I had just stowed my luggage and settled myself in a seat when there was a tap on the window, and I looked up and saw a man standing outside, carrying a briefcase in one hand and a bunch of flowers in the other.

It was, astonishingly, Nigel.

I got up and went back to the door and stepped down onto the platform. He was walking towards me, smiling sheepishly.

"Prue. I thought I wouldn't find you."

"What on earth are you doing here?"

"I came to see you off. Wish you bon voyage." He held out the bunch of flowers, which were small and shaggy yellow chrysanthemums. "And to bring you these."

I was, despite myself, very touched. I recognised that his coming here to the station was a generous

gesture of forgiveness, and to make it clear that he
had understood why I was letting him down. This
had the effect of making me feel more of a heel
than ever. I took the flowers in their collar of crisp
white paper and buried my nose in them. They
smelt delicious. I looked up at him and smiled.

"It's ten o'clock. Oughtn't you to be at your
desk by now?"

He shook his head. "No hurry."

"I didn't realise you were so high up in the
banking world."

Nigel grinned. "I'm not, but I don't exactly
have to clock in. Anyway, made a phone call. Said
I'd been held up." He had a solid, mature sort of
face, with fair hair beginning to thin on top, but
when he grinned like that, he looked quite boyish. I began to wonder if I was mad, abandoning
this personable man in order to go and nurse my
unpredictable aunt Phoebe. Perhaps my mother
had been right, after all.

I said, "I'm sorry about letting you down. I
wrote to your mother last night."

"Perhaps, another time . . ." said Nigel gener-
ously. "Anyway, keep in touch. Let me know
when you get back to London."

I knew that he would be waiting for me, if I
asked him. Ready to meet my train, to drive me

back to Islington, to pick up the threads of our relationship as though I had never been away.

"I'll do that."

"I hope your aunt recovers quickly."

"It's only a broken arm. She's not ill."

There came a short, uncomfortable pause. Then Nigel said, "Well . . ." He moved forward to kiss my cheek. It was more of a peck than a kiss. "Good-bye, and have a good journey."

"Thank you for coming. Thank you for the flowers."

He stepped back, made an indeterminate gesture of farewell, turned and walked away. I watched him go, making his way through the shifting confusion of porters, barrows, families with suitcases. At the barrier he turned back for a final time. We waved. Then he was gone. I got back into the train, stowed the flowers in the luggage rack and sat down once more. I wished that he had not come.

I was very much a Shackleton, but every now and then stray emotions would float to the surface of my mind, which I recognised as stemming straight from my mother. This was just such a time. I must be mad not to want to be with Nigel, to become involved with him, even to spend the rest of my life with him. Normally, I bucked like a horse at the very idea of settling down, but at this moment, sitting in the train, gazing out the window at Paddington Station, it suddenly seemed enormously attractive. Security; that's what this dependable man would give me. I imagined living in his solid London house, going to Scotland for my holidays; only working if I wanted to, and not because I needed the money. I thought about having children . . .

A voice said, "I'm sorry, is this seat taken?"

"What . . . ?" I looked up and saw the man standing there in the aisle between the seats. He carried a small suitcase, and there was a child beside him, a small thin girl about ten years old, dark haired and wearing round, owllike spectacles.

"No, it's not taken."

He said, "Good," and lifted the suitcase up into the rack. He did not look in the mood for any sort of pleasantry, and a certain impatience of manner made me not ask him to watch out for my bunch of chrysanthemums. He was dressed, as Nigel had been, for some City office, in a navy chalk-striped suit. But the suit sat ill upon him, as though he had lately put on a good deal of weight (I imagined enormous expense-account luncheons), and as he reached up with the suitcase, I had a direct view of his expensive, bulging shirt and straining buttons. He was dark, and once, perhaps, had been good-looking, but now his jowls were heavy, his complexion florid, and his greying hair worn long on the back of his collar, possibly to atone for the lack of it on top.

"There you are," he said to the little girl. "Go on, sit down."

She did so, cautiously, perched on the very edge of the seat. She carried a single comic paper and wore a red leather purse slung by a strap across one shoulder. She was a pale child, with hair cut very short, exposing a long and slender neck. This, and her spectacles, and her expression of stoic misery gave her the appearance of a small boy, and I was reminded of other small boys I had observed on station platforms, dwarfed by stiff new uniforms, fighting tears, and being told by beefy fathers how much they were going to enjoy being at boarding school.

"Got your ticket all right?"

She nodded.

"Granny'll meet you at the junction."

She nodded again.

"Well . . ." He ran a hand back over his head. He was obviously longing to be off. "That's it, then. You'll be all right."

Once more she nodded. They looked, unsmiling, at each other. He began to move away and then remembered something else.

"Here . . ." He felt in his breast pocket, produced a crocodile wallet, a ten-pound note. "You'll need something to eat. When it's time, take yourself along to the restaurant car and get some lunch."

She took the ten-pound note and sat looking at it.

"Good-bye, then."

"Good-bye."

He went. At the window he paused to wave and give a cursory smile. Then he disappeared, hurrying in the direction of some sleek, showy car that would restore him to the safe, masculine world of his business.

As I had already told myself that Nigel was nice, I now told myself that this man was horrible and wondered why such an unengaging person had been given the job of seeing the little girl off. She sat beside me, still as a mouse. After a little she reached for her handbag, undid the zipper, put the ten-pound note inside, and shut the zipper again. I thought about saying something friendly to her, but there was a shine of tears in her eyes behind the spectacles, so I decided, for the moment, to leave well alone. A moment later the train started to move, and we were off.

I opened my *Times*, read the headlines and all the gloomy news, and then turned with a pleasant sensation of relief to the Arts page. I found what I was looking for, which was the review of an exhibition that had opened a couple of days before in the Peter Chastal Gallery, which was only a couple of doors away from where I worked for Marcus Bernstein.

The artist was a young man called Daniel Cassens, and I had always been interested in his career because, when he was about twenty, he had spent a year in Cornwall living with Phoebe and studying sculpture with Chips. I had never met him, but Phoebe and Chips had become very fond of him, and when he left them to continue his career in America, Phoebe had followed his progress avidly and enthusiastically as if he had been her own son.

He had travelled and spent some years in America and then had taken himself on to Japan, where he had engrossed himself in the intricate simplicities of Oriental art.

This latest exhibition was a direct outcome of his years in Japan, and the critic was enthusiastic, revelling in the tranquillity and formality of Daniel Cassens's work, praising the controlled brushwork of the watercolours, the subtlety of detail.

". . . This is a unique collection," he finished his piece. "The paintings are complementary, each one a single facet of a total and rare experience. Take an hour or so off from your daily round and visit the Chastal Gallery. You will certainly not be disappointed."

Phoebe would be delighted, and I was glad for her. I closed the paper and looked out the window and saw that we had left the suburbs behind and were now out into the country. It was a damp day, with large grey clouds rolling across the sky, revealing every now and then a patch of limpid blue. Trees were beginning to turn, the first leaves to fall. There were tractors ploughing out in the fields, and cottage gardens, as we rocketed past, were purple with Michaelmas daisies.

I remembered my small companion and turned to see how she was getting on. She had not yet opened her comic or unbuttoned her coat, but the tears had receded and she seemed a little more composed.

"Where are you going to?" I asked her.

She said, "Cornwall."

"I'm going to Cornwall, too. Whereabouts are you going?"

"I'm going to stay with my grandmother."

"That'll be nice." I thought about this. "But isn't it term time? Shouldn't you be at school?"

"Yes, I should. I'm at a boarding school. We all went back, and then the boiler blew up, so they closed the school for a week till it's mended and sent us all home again."

"How terrible. I hope nobody was hurt."

"No. But Miss Brownrigg, our headmistress, had to go to bed for a day. Matron said it was shock."

"I'm not surprised."

"So I went home, but there's nobody there but my father. My mother's on holiday in Majorca. She went at the end of the holidays. So I've got to go to Granny."

She didn't make it sound a very attractive prospect. I was trying to think of something comforting to say to jolly her along when she picked up her comic and settled down, rather pointedly, to read it. I was amused but took the hint, found my book, and began to read. The journey progressed in silence until the waiter from the restaurant car made his way down the train to tell us that luncheon was being served.

I laid down my book. "Are you going to go and have some lunch?" I asked her, knowing about the ten-pound note in her bag.

She looked agonised. "I . . . I don't know which way to go."

"I'm going. Would you like to come with me? We could have lunch together."

Her expression changed to one of grateful relief. "Oh, could I? I've got the money, but I've never been on a train by myself before, and I don't know what I'm meant to do."

"I know, it's muddling, isn't it? Come along, let's go before all the tables get booked up."

Together we made our way down the lurching corridors, found the restaurant car, and were shown to a table for two. There was a fresh white cloth, and flowers in a glass carafe.

She said, "I'm a bit hot. Do you think I could take off my coat?"

"I think that would be a good idea."

She did this, and the waiter came to help her, and fold the coat, and lay it over the back of her seat. We opened the menus.

"Are you feeling hungry?" I asked her.

"Yes I am. We had breakfast *ages* ago."

"Where do you live?"

"In Sunningdale. I came up to London with my father in his car. He drives up every morning."

"Your . . . ? Was that your father who saw you off?"

"Yes." He hadn't even kissed her good-bye. "He works in an office in the City." Our eyes met, and then she looked hastily away. "He doesn't like being late."

I said, soothingly, "Few men do. Is it his mother you're going to stay with?"

"No. Granny's my mother's mother."

I said, sounding chatty, "I'm going to stay with an aunt. She's broken her arm, and she can't drive her car, so I'm going to look after her. She lives at the very end of Cornwall in a village called Penmarron."

"Penmarron? But I'm going to Penmarron too."

This was a coincidence. "How extraordinary."

"I'm Charlotte Collis. I'm Mrs. Tolliver's granddaughter. She's my granny. Do you know Mrs. Tolliver?"

"Yes, I do. Not very well, but I do know her. My mother used to play bridge with her. And my aunt is called Phoebe Shackleton."

And now her face lit up. For the first time since I had set eyes on her, she looked a natural and excited child. Her eyes were wide behind the spectacles, and her mouth opened in a delighted gasp of surprise, revealing teeth too big for her narrow face.

"*Phoebe!* Phoebe's my best friend. I go and have tea with her and things, every time I go and stay with Granny. I didn't know she'd broken her arm." She gazed into my face. "You . . . you're not Prue, are you?"

I smiled. "Yes, I am. How did you know?"

"I *thought* I knew your face. I've seen your photograph in Phoebe's sitting room. I always thought you looked *lovely.*"

"Thank you."

"And Phoebe used to tell me about you when I went to see her. It's lovely going to tea with her, because it's not like being with a grown-up person and I'm allowed to go on my own. And we always play with the carousel that used to be a gramophone."

"That was mine. Chips made it for me."

"I never knew Chips. He was dead before I can remember."

"And I," I told her, "never knew your mother."

"But we go and stay with Granny most summers."

"And I am usually there at Easter, or sometimes

for Christmas, so our paths have never crossed. I don't think I even know her name."

"It's Annabelle. She was Annabelle Tolliver. But she's called Mrs. Collis now."

"And do you have brothers and sisters?"

"One brother. Michael. He's fifteen. He's at Wellington."

"And the boiler at Wellington hasn't blown up?"

It was an attempt to add a little levity to the conversation, but Charlotte did not smile. She said, "No."

I studied the menu and thought about Mrs. Tolliver. My memories of her were of a tall, elegant, and rather chilling lady, always immaculately turned out, her grey hair neatly groomed, her skirts pleated and pressed, her long, narrow shoes polished like chestnuts. I thought of White Lodge, where Charlotte was going to stay, and wondered what a child would find to do in those neatly manicured gardens, that quiet and orderly house.

I looked across the table at the child and saw that she, too, with furrowed brow, was trying to decide what she would have for lunch. She seemed a sad little person. It couldn't have been much fun, being sent home from school simply because the boiler there had blown up. Unexpected and probably unwanted, with your mother abroad and no person to take care of you. It couldn't have been much fun, being put by yourself on a train and shunted off to the end of the country to visit your grandmother. I wished, all at once, for Mrs. Tolliver to be dumpy and cozy, with a round, warm bosom and a passion for knitting dolls' clothes and playing Clock Patience.

Charlotte looked up and saw me watching her. She sighed hopelessly. "I don't know what I want."

I said, "A moment ago you told me you were feeling very hungry. Why don't you have everything?"

"All right." She decided on vegetable soup, roast beef, and ice cream. "And do you think," she added wistfully, "there might be enough money over for a Coca-Cola?"

What is there so magical about travelling by train to Cornwall? I know I am not the first person to have known the enchantment as the line crosses the Tamar by the old Brunel railway bridge, as though one were entering the gates of some marvellous foreign country. Each time I go I tell myself that it cannot be the same, but it always is. And it is impossible to pinpoint the exact reasons for this euphoria. The shapes of the houses, perhaps, pinkwashed in the evening sun. The smallness of the fields; the lofty viaducts soaring over deep, wooded valleys; the first distant glimpses of the sea? Or perhaps the saintly names of small stations that we rocket through and leave behind, or the voices of the porters on the platform at Truro?

We reached St. Abbatt's Junction at a quarter to five. As the train drew alongside the platform, Charlotte and I were ready by the door, with our suitcases and my bunch of chrysanthemums, by now distinctly worse for wear. When we stepped down from the train, we were assailed by a blustering west wind, and I could smell the sea, salty and strong. There were palm trees on the platform, rattling their leaves like old, broken umbrellas, and a porter opened the door of the guards' van and manhandled out of it a crate of indignant hens.

I knew that Mr. Thomas was going to come and meet me. Mr. Thomas owned the only taxi in Penmarron, and Phoebe had told me over the telephone that she had engaged his services. As we walked up towards the bridge, I saw Mr. Thomas waiting, bundled up in an overcoat as though it were winter and wearing on his head the hat that he had bought at a jumble sale and that had once belonged to some noble chauffeur. When he was not driving a taxi, he was a pig farmer, and for this occupation he had another hat, felt, and of great antiquity. Phoebe, who had a Rabelaisian wit, once wondered what sort of hat he wore when he was getting into bed with Mrs. Thomas, but my mother had pursed her lips and lowered her eyes and refused to be amused, so Phoebe had not wondered it again.

There was no sign of Mrs. Tolliver. I could feel Charlotte's anxiety.

"Perhaps your grandmother's waiting on the other side of the bridge."

The train, which never stopped long anywhere, drew out. We scanned the opposite platform, but the only person who waited was a fat lady with a shopping bag. Not Mrs. Tolliver.

"Maybe she's sitting in the car in the station yard. It's a cold evening to be standing about."

"I hope she hasn't forgotten," said Charlotte.

But Mr. Thomas was to reassure us. "Hello, my dear," he said to me, coming to meet us and to relieve me of my case. "How are you? Nice to see you again. Have a good journey, did you?" He looked down at Charlotte. "You're Mrs. Tolliver's little girl, aren't you. That's right. My orders are to pick up the pair of you. Take the little girl to White Lodge, and then you on to Miss Shackleton's. Travel together, did you?"

"Yes, we did; we met on the train."

"Your aunt would have come, but she can't drive her car with that dratted arm of hers. Come on now," he turned to Charlotte, "give me your case, too, easier to carry two than one . . ."

And thus burdened, he trudged up the wooden steps and over the bridge, and Charlotte and I followed him. Settled in his taxi, which had molting leather seats and always smelt faintly of pig, I said, "I hope Mrs. Tolliver hasn't broken her arm, too."

"Oh, no, she's lovely." In Cornwall, lovely means well. "Nothing wrong with her. But didn't seem much point two cars coming . . ." And with that he started up his engine, and the taxi, after backfiring twice, ground into gear and shot forward up the hill that led to the main road.

I sat back and felt annoyed. Perhaps it was the most sensible thing to do, arranging for Charlotte and me to share the taxi, but it would have been more welcoming if Mrs. Tolliver had come to the station to meet Charlotte herself. It was, after all, a drive of only two miles. Charlotte was looking away from me, out the window, and I suspected that once more she was fighting tears. I didn't blame her.

"That was a good idea, wasn't it, for us to share the taxi?" I tried to sound enthusiastic, as though I approved.

She did not turn round. She said, "I suppose so."

However, we had arrived. We were here. Along the main road on that windy afternoon, and down the hill beneath the oak trees. Past the gates of what used to be the Squire's house, and then into the village. Nothing ever seemed to change. Up the hill again, past the cottages and the shops, an old man walking his dog, the petrol station, the pub. We turned down the road that led to the church and the sea, the copse of ancient oaks, the farm with its slated steadings, and so to the open white gates of White Lodge.

Mr. Thomas changed down with a hideous clash of gears and turned into these gates. We came up the short drive, between overhanging trees, and I saw the swept verges and the fading banks of hydrangea. We rounded a clump of these and drew up on the gravel sweep in front of the house. It was a stone house, whitewashed and solid. A wisteria clambered up the wall to the up-stairs windows, and a flight of stone steps rose to the closed front door. We all got out of the taxi, and Mr. Thomas went up the steps to ring the bell. The wind suddenly blew up a gust and swept a scatter of dead leaves into a whirlpool at our feet. After a short wait, the door was opened and Mrs. Tolliver appeared. She looked just the same as I had remembered her and came down the steps towards us with her smoothly coiffed grey hair and her slender, elegant figure. Her face was neatly arranged in a smile of welcome.

"Charlotte. Well, here you are." She stooped to kiss the child briskly. She straightened up. I am tall, but she was taller. "Prue. How very nice to see you. I hope you didn't mind sharing the taxi."

"We didn't mind in the least. We met on the train in London, so we've travelled all the way together."

"How very nice. Now, Charlotte, is this your suitcase? In you come. There's just time to wash your hands, and then we'll have tea. Mrs. Curnow's made a sponge cake. I expect you like sponge cake."

Charlotte said, "Yes." It did not sound convincing. She probably hated sponge cake. She would much have preferred fish fingers and chips.

". . . And Prue, I hope you find Phoebe well.

29

Perhaps you'll come for lunch one day. How is your mother?"

"She's well."

"I'll get all the news some other time. Come along now, Charlotte."

"Good-bye," Charlotte said to me.

"Good-bye, Charlotte. Come and see us."

"Yes, I will."

I waited by the taxi until they had gone up the steps and through the door. Mrs. Tolliver carried the suitcase, and Charlotte, still clutching her comic, trod cautiously at her heels. She did not turn to wave. The door closed behind them.

Chapter 2

I⟁ SEEMED ALL WRONG that Charlotte should have
been given a reception of such little warmth,
while I, twenty-three years old and perfectly able
to stand on my own two feet, had Holly Cottage
waiting for me, and Phoebe. At Holly Cottage
there was no driveway; just a patch of gravel between the gate and the house. At Holly Cottage
the garden was a mass of dahlias and chrysanthemums, the front door stood open to the evening
breeze, and from an upstairs window a pink cotton curtain blew in the wind, like a person waving
a cheerful greeting. No sooner was the taxi turning in at her gate than Phoebe herself appeared.
Her left arm was strapped up in a bulky white

plaster cast, but her right arm signalled its own exuberant welcome, and she came running forward so unexpectedly that Mr. Thomas very nearly ran her over.

Before the car had stopped, I was out of it and into Phoebe's one-armed embrace. The one I gave back to her did double duty for both of us.

"Oh, my darling," she crowed, "what an angel. Never thought you'd be able to come. Couldn't believe it. I'm going nearly insane trying to get myself about. Can't even ride a bicycle . . ."

Laughing, I let her go, and we stood back and looked at each other with the greatest of satisfaction. Looking at Phoebe is always a pleasure. Unpredictable, but always a pleasure. She was at that time well into her sixties, but it has always been impossible to equate Phoebe to the passing years.

I saw the thick stockings, the stout boots, the worn and faded blue-jean skirt. Over these she wore a man's shirt and cardigan (probably inherited from Chips); there were gold chains about her neck, and a tartan scarf, and on her head, inevitably, a hat.

She always wore hats, broad-brimmed, deep-crowned, rather dashing. She had taken to wearing them to protect her eyes, while painting out of doors, from the cold, white glare of the Cornish light, and they had become so much part of her that she very often forgot to take them off. This one was a rich brown, decorated with grey gull feathers stuck into the ribbon band. Beneath its kindly shade, Phoebe's face, the skin netted with lines, twinkled and smiled at me. The smile revealed teeth that were even and white as a child's, and her eyes were the deepest speedwell blue, their brightness challenged only by the turquoise-and-silver earrings that dangled on either side of her face.

I said, "You're a fraud. You may have broken your arm, but you're as beautiful as ever."

"What rubbish! Do you hear that, Mr. Thomas, she says I'm beautiful. She must be either mad or blind. Now, what's this? Your suitcase. And what are the dead flowers for? I don't want any dead flowers . . ." Holding the poor things, she began to laugh again. "Now, Mr. Thomas, you'll have to send me a bill. I can't pay you just now—I've mislaid my handbag."

"I'll pay, Phoebe."

"Of course you won't. Mr. Thomas doesn't mind, do you, Mr. Thomas?"

Mr. Thomas assured her that he didn't. He got back into his taxi, but Phoebe pursued him in order to put her head through the window and ask after Mrs. Thomas's bad leg. Mr. Thomas be-gan to tell her, at some length. Halfway through his dissertation, Phoebe decided she'd had enough. "So glad she's better," she said firmly, and withdrew her head from the window. Mr. Thomas, halted in full spate, was not in the least disconcerted. It was just Miss Shackleton, and heaven only knew, she had some funny ways. The old taxi was set into motion once more and the next moment had sped away, scattering gravel through the gate and up the road.

"Now." Phoebe took my arm. "Let's get in-doors. I want to hear all the news."

Together we went through the open door and into the house. I stood in the hall, looked about, and loved everything for being the same. I saw the polished floors scattered with rugs; the un-carpeted wooden staircase that led to the upper floor; the whitewashed walls hung, haphazard, with Phoebe's tiny, jewel-bright oil paintings.

The house smelt of turpentine and wood smoke and linseed oil and garlic and roses, but its great-est charm was the effect of airy lightness engen-dered by pale colours, lacy curtains, straw rugs, and polished wood. Even in the middle of winter, it always felt summery.

I took a deep breath, savouring it all. "Heaven," I said. "Heaven to be back."

"You're in the same old room," said Phoebe and then left me, heading for the kitchen. I knew she would spend some time trying to resuscitate Nigel's poor flowers, even though she had more than enough of her own. I picked up my case and went upstairs to the room that had been mine since I was a very small girl. I opened the door and was assailed by a gust of cold air pouring in from the wide open window. I shut the door, and everything stopped billowing. Putting down my case, I went to the window and leaned out to gaze at the familiar view.

The tide was out, and the evening smelt of seaweed. You were never far from the sea smells at Holly Cottage, because the house had been built on a grassy bluff overlooking a tidal estuary, which penetrated inland like a huge lake and was filled and emptied each day by the tides.

Below the house was a wide seawall, where once a single-line railway siding had led to a busy shipyard. The shipyard was closed now and the railway sleepers removed, but the wall still stood, solid as a cliff. At high tide the water reached nearly to the rim of this wall, and in summer it made a good place to swim, but at low tide there was nothing but acres of empty sand, with a few weedy rocks and shallow pools scattered here and there and a dozen or so derelict fishing boats that had been pulled up on the shingle winters ago and for some reason never floated again.

On this, the south side of the house, the garden was unexpectedly large. An irregularly shaped lawn, edged here and there with random flower beds, sloped down to a boundary hedge of escallonia. In the middle of this was a gate, and over the gate the clipped escallonia had been trimmed into an arch, which gave the garden a charmingly formal and old-fashioned aspect. To the right, beyond a high brick wall, where Chips Armitage used to grow peach trees, was a sizeable vegetable garden, and at the bottom of this, scarcely visible from the house, he had built his studio. All I could see was the pitch of the slate roof and, sitting on it, a single herring gull. As I watched, it spread its wings, screaming defiance at nothing in particular, and then took flight, soaring and gliding away, out over the wet, empty sands.

I smiled, closed the window against the cold, and went down to Phoebe.

We sat facing each other across the hearth rug, with a blazing log fire to warm us, and the light outside gradually dying into evening. There was a big brown teapot on the trolley, hand-painted earthenware cups and saucers, a plate of fresh scones, yellow farm butter, and homemade cherry jam.

"You didn't make these scones, Phoebe. You couldn't, with only one hand."

"No, Lily Tonkins made them this morning. Darling woman, she comes in every day, and she's simply taken over the kitchen. I never realised what a marvellous cook she is."

"But how did you break your arm?"

"Oh, my dear, too stupid. I was down in the studio looking for some old folios of Chips's . . . I knew they were on the top shelf of his bookcase, and I stood on a chair, and of course some worm, unknown to me, had burrowed into the wood, and the leg gave way, and down I came!" She roared with laughter as though it were the best joke in the world. She was still wearing her feathered hat. "Very lucky not to break my leg. I came back to the house, and by great good fortune there was the postman, delivering the afternoon mail. So I hopped in beside him and he drove me to the cottage hospital and they tied me up in this tiresome cast."

"You poor thing."

"Oh, never mind, it doesn't hurt much; it's just

a nuisance, and maddening not being able to drive. I've got to go back to the hospital tomorrow to let the doctor see it . . . I suppose he thinks I'm going to get gangrene or something . . ."

"I'll drive you . . ."

"You won't have to, because they're sending an ambulance. I've never been in an ambulance before. I'm rather looking forward to it. Now, how's Delia?"

Delia was my mother. I said she was well.

"And what sort of a train journey did you have?" Before I could tell her, she remembered the arrangement she had made with Mrs. Tolliver. "Heavens, I forgot to ask about Charlotte Collis. Did Mr. Thomas remember to collect her at the station as well?"

"Yes."

"How fortunate. I hope you didn't mind sharing the ride with her. Personally, I thought Mrs. Tolliver might have gone to fetch the poor child herself, but she seemed to think it was pointless if Mr. Thomas was going anyway."

"I thought she might have come to meet her, too."

"How is she, poor little mite?"

"She seemed a bit anxious. Not at all excited at

the thought of staying with her grandmother. The only person she showed any enthusiasm for was you. She adores you."

"It's funny, isn't it. You'd think she'd rather be with children of her own age. Except that there aren't many children in this village, and even if there were, she's always been something of a loner. The first time we met, I found her wandering on the beach by herself. She said she was out for a walk, so I asked her back for tea and rang Mrs. Tolliver to say she was with me. After that she came quite often. She's fascinated by my pictures and paints and sketchbooks. I gave her a sketch pad and some felt pens for herself, and she has a remarkable talent and a marvellous imagination. Then she loves being told stories; hearing about Chips and all the stupid things he and I used to do together. Extraordinary, really, in such a young child."

I said, "You know, I don't think I ever knew that Mrs. Tolliver had a grandchild. I don't think I ever realised that she had a daughter. Or a husband, for that matter. What happened to Mr. Tolliver?"

"He died, some years ago. When Chips and I first came here, he was still alive, and they lived in great style. You know the sort of thing—a Bentley in the garage and two gardeners and a cook and a housemaid. Annabelle was impossibly spoiled and indulged—a real only child. But then Mr. Tolliver had a heart attack—keeled over on the seventh green of the golf course—and never recovered. After that nothing was quite the same again. Of course, Mrs. Tolliver never said anything—she's the most reserved woman I know—but the big car was sold and a general cutting back rather obviously took place. Annabelle had been sent to some ridiculously expensive school in Switzerland, and she had to leave and come home and attend the local Comprehensive. She simply hated it. I think she felt that life had deliberately humiliated her. Silly girl."

"What was she like?"

"Very beautiful, but without the vestige of a brain. After she was married and had her little boy, she used to come down for the summers and stay with her mother, and every time there were three or four lovelorn fellows dancing attendance. At a party you couldn't see her for men. Just like bees round a honey pot."

"She's in Majorca just now. Charlotte told me that much."

"I know. I've heard all about that. I think Mrs. Tolliver rather felt that she should come back and look after Charlotte herself. She was annoyed about the school boiler blowing up. She felt it was inefficient. I was horrified. It might have killed all the children. But Mrs. Tolliver was far more concerned at the prospect of having Charlotte to stay."

"But doesn't she like Charlotte?"

"Oh, I think she quite likes her," Phoebe told me in her airy way. "But she's never been interested in children, and I think she finds Charlotte very dull. And, as well, she's never had the child on her own before. I think she's wondering what on earth she's going to do with her."

Outside, the wind was getting up, rattling the window sashes and whistling around the corners of the house. It was nearly dark, but the room in which we sat was warm with dancing firelight. I reached for the kettle that simmered on a brass hob near the flames and refilled the teapot.

"What about Annabelle's husband?"

"Leslie Collis? I could never stand him, gruesome man."

"I thought he was gruesome, too. He didn't even kiss Charlotte good-bye. How did Annabelle meet him?"

"He was staying at the Castle Hotel in Porthkerris with three other stockbrokers, or whatever it is he does in the City. I don't know how they met, but the moment he set eyes on her, that was it."

"He couldn't have been attractive."

"In a funny way, he was. He had a certain sort of dark, flashy charm. Spent money like water, drove around in a Ferrari."

"Do you think Annabelle was in love with him?"

"Not for a moment. Annabelle was in love only with herself. But he could give her everything that she'd ever wanted, and she didn't like being poor. And of course Mrs. Tolliver encouraged it madly. I don't think she ever forgave her poor husband for leaving her in straitened circumstances, and she was determined that Annabelle should marry well."

I thought about this. Then I poured myself another cup of tea and lay back against the cushions of the deep and friendly old chair. I said, "I suppose all mothers are the same."

"Don't tell me Delia's been at you again."

"Oh, no, she's not been at me. But there's this man . . . he brought me those chrysanthemums . . ." And I told her about Nigel Gordon and the invitation to Scotland.

Phoebe listened sympathetically, and when I

had finished, she said, "I think he sounds very nice."

"He is. That's the trouble. He's terribly nice. But my mother's already got wedding bells banging to and fro and keeps reminding me that I'm twenty-three and ought to be settling down. Perhaps if she didn't go on about it so, I might marry him."

"You mustn't marry him unless you can't imagine life without him."

"That's just it. I can. Quite easily."

"We all need different things from life. Your mother needs security. That's why she married your father, and a fat lot of good it did her, because she never took the time to get to know him before she made that spectacular entrance up the aisle. But you're a special person. You need more than a man to bring you flowers and pay the bills. You're intelligent and you're talented. And when you do settle down with a man, it is absolutely vital that he makes you laugh. Chips and I laughed all the time, even when we were poor and unsuccessful and didn't know how we were going to pay the grocer's bill. We were always laughing."

I smiled, remembering them together. I said, "Talking of Chips, did you know that Daniel Cassens has an exhibition on at the Chastal Gallery? I read a rave review in the *Times* this morning."

"I read it too. So exciting. Dear, clever boy. I intended going up to London for the opening day, but then I went and broke this stupid arm and the doctor said I wasn't to travel."

"Is he in London? Daniel, I mean."

"Heaven knows where he is. Probably still in Japan. Or Mexico, or somewhere mad. But I'd love to see that exhibition. Perhaps, if I'm able, I'll come back to London with you and we'll go together. What fun that would be! Something to look forward to."

That night I had a dream. I was on some island —a tropical island, palm-fringed and white-sanded. It was very hot. I was on a beach, walking down towards the silent, glass-clear sea. I meant to swim, but the water, when I reached it, was only inches deep, scarcely covering my ankles. I walked for a long time, and then, all at once, the sand fell steeply away, and I was out of my depth, swimming, and the water was dark as ink and the current like a rushing river. I felt myself borne along on its flow, towards the horizon. I knew that I should turn back, swim for the beach, but the current was too strong, and there was no resisting it. So I stopped fighting and let myself be carried along, knowing that I could never return, but so marvellous was the sensation of going with the tide that I did not care.

I woke with the dream still sharp and clear in my mind. I could remember every detail of it. I lay in bed, thinking about the clear water and the sensation of peace as I was borne along in the wash of that warm and tranquil sea. All dreams have meaning, and I wondered how some professional would analyse this one. It occurred to me, in an unworried sort of way, that it might be about dying.

Chapter 3

THE EARLY MORNING turned into a beautiful day. Breezy and bright, the blue sky was patched with large, sailing white clouds blown in from the Atlantic. The sun blinked in and out of these clouds, and during the morning the flood tide slowly filled the estuary, creeping up the sands, filling the tide pools, and finally, by about eleven o'clock, reaching the seawall below the house.

Phoebe had gone to keep her appointment at the Cottage Hospital, borne there in some style by the local ambulance. For the trip she had donned yet another hat, black velours, bound by a tussore scarf, and she had waved enthusiastically through the open window as though she were setting off on a jaunt. She would be back for lunch. I had offered to prepare this, but Lily Tonkins, already busy with the vacuum cleaner, said that she already had a bit of lamb in the oven, so I found a sketch pad and a stick of charcoal, stole an apple from the fruit bowl, and took myself out of doors.

And now, at eleven o'clock, I sat on the grassy slope above the seawall, with the sun a dazzle on the wind-ruffled waters of the estuary and the morning freshness filled with the scream of gulls. I had done a rough sketch of the derelict fishing boats with their ramshackle chains and anchors, their empty masts piercing the sky. As I filled in some detail of a weather-scarred hatchway, I heard the morning train from Porthkerris come through the cutting behind Holly Cottage and draw up at the little halt by the edge of the shore. It was a very small and infrequent train, and a moment or two later it gave a hoot and moved on again, around the curve of the line and out of sight.

So engrossed was I in maddening perspectives that I was scarcely aware of this happening, but when I next looked up to study the keel of an upended dinghy, a movement caught the corner of my eye. I looked and saw a solitary figure walking towards me. He approached from the direction of the station, and I presumed that he had alighted from the train, crossed the line, and so followed the track of the disused siding. There was nothing unusual about this. People often took the train from Porthkerris to Penmarron and then walked back to Porthkerris, following the foot-path that led for three miles or more along the edge of the cliff.

I lost interest in my drawing. I laid down the sketch pad, picked up my apple, and began to eat it. I watched the stranger's progress. He was a tall man, long-legged, with an easy, loping stride. His clothes at first were simply a blur of blue and white, but as he came closer I saw that he wore denim jeans and a faded shirt, and over this a white knitted jacket, the sort that people bring home from holidays in Ireland. The jacket was unbuttoned, flying open in the wind, and a red and white handkerchief, like a gipsy's, was knot-ted around his throat. His head was bare, his hair very dark, and though he did not appear to be in any sort of hurry, he was covering the ground at considerable pace.

He looked, I decided, a man who knew where he was going.

Now he had come to the far end of the seawall. Here he paused and looked out over the dazzling water, shielding his eyes from the glare. A moment later he moved on once more, and it was then that he spied me, sitting there in the long grass, eating my apple, watching him.

I thought that he would probably walk past me, perhaps with a casual "good morning," but as he drew level with me, he stopped and stood there, with his back to the water, his hands in the pockets of that voluminous jacket, his head tilted back. A gust of wind ruffled his dark hair. He said, "Hello."

His voice was boyish, his demeanour youthful, but his thin, brown face was not a boy's face, and there were strong lines etched around his mouth and his deeply set eyes.

"Hello."

"What a lovely morning."

"Isn't it?" I finished my apple and tossed the core away. A gull instantly pounced on it and bore it off to consume in private.

"I just got off the train."

"I thought you must have. Are you going to walk back to Porthkerris?"

"No, as a matter of fact, I'm not." And with that he began to climb the grassy slope, picking his way between the bramble patches and the clumps of bracken. When he reached my side, he collapsed, a sprawl of long boney limbs. I saw his old canvas shoes had holes in the toes, and the warmth of the sun made his jacket smell sheepy, as though it had been knitted straight off some oily fleece.

I said, "You can walk by the cliffs if you want to."

"Ah, but then you see, I don't want to." He spied my sketch pad and before I could stop him had picked it up. "That's very nice."

I hate people looking at my work, especially when it's not even finished. "It's just a scribble."

"Not at all." He surveyed it for a moment longer and then laid it down without further comment. He said, "There is a deadly fascination about watching a flood tide. Is that what you've been doing?"

"For the past hour."

He felt in his capacious pocket and brought out a thin packet of cigars, a book of matches, and a dog-eared paperback, obviously much read and consulted. Interest stirred when I saw that it was *Vanishing Cornwall* by Daphne du Maurier. The book of matches had "The Castle Hotel Porthkerris" printed upon it. I felt like a detective and as though, already, I knew quite a lot about him.

He selected a cigar and lit it. His hands were beautiful; long and narrow, with spade-tipped fingers. On one wrist he wore a cheap and un-remarkable watch, on the other a chain of gold links, very old-looking and heavy.

As he put the matches and the cigars back into his pocket, I said, "Are you staying at the Castle?"

He looked up in surprise and then smiled. "How did you guess that?"

"Deduction. Matches. Sharp eyes."

"Of course. How stupid of me. Well, I spent last night there, if you can call that staying. I came down from London yesterday."

"So did I. I came by train."

"I wish I had. I got a lift. I hate driving. Hate cars. I'd much rather sit and look out of the window or read a book. Infinitely more civilized." He settled himself into a more comfortable position, leaning on an elbow. "Are you on holiday, or staying here, or is this where you live?"

"Just staying."

"In the village?"

"Yes. Right here, actually."

"What do you mean by right here?"

"In the house up there."

"Holly Cottage." He began to laugh. "Are you staying with Phoebe?"

"Do you know Phoebe?"

"Of course I know Phoebe. That's why I'm here. To see her."

"Well you won't find her just now, because she's gone to the Cottage Hospital in an ambulance." He looked horrified. "It's all right, she hasn't had a stroke or anything, just broken her arm. It's been put in a cast, and the doctor wants to have a look at it."

"Well, that's a relief. Is she all right?"

"Of course. She'll be back for lunch."

"And who are you? A nurse, or one of her perpetual students?"

"No, I'm a perpetual niece."

"You wouldn't by any chance be Prue?"

"Yes, I would." I frowned. "But who are you?"

"Daniel Cassens."

I said, ridiculously, "But you're in Mexico."

"Mexico? Never been to Mexico in my life."

"Phoebe said you were probably in Mexico or somewhere mad."

"That was charitable of her. In fact, I've been in the Virgin Islands, on a boat with some American friends, but then somebody said there was going to be a hurricane, so I decided the time was ripe to get out. But back in New York, I was instantly bombarded with cables from Peter Chastal to say I had to be in London for the opening day of this exhibition he's mounted for me."

"I know about that. You see, I work for Marcus Bernstein. We're practically next door to Peter Chastal. And I read the reviews of your exhibition. I think you've got a success on your hands. Phoebe read it, too. She was enormously thrilled."

"She would be."

"Were you at the opening?"

"Yes, I was. I finally made it. At the last moment I gave in and caught a flight over."

"Why were you so reluctant? Most people wouldn't miss it for anything. All the champagne and the adulation."

"I hate my own exhibitions. It's the most ghastly form of exposure, like putting one's children on display. All those eyes, staring. Makes me feel quite ill."

I understood. "But you did go?"

"Yes, for a little. But I wore a disguise—dark glasses and a concealing hat. I looked like an insane sort of spy. I only stayed for half an hour, and then when Peter wasn't looking, I slunk away and went and sat in a pub and tried to decide what to do next. And then I got talking to this man, and I bought him a beer, and he said that he was driving to Cornwall, so I hitched a lift with him and arrived last night."

"Why didn't you come and stay with Phoebe?"

Without thinking I asked the question and immediately wished that I hadn't. He looked away from me, pulled at a tuft of grass with his hand, and let the wind blow it from his fingers.

"I don't know," he said at last. "So many reasons. Some high-minded, some not so."

"You know she would have welcomed you."

"Yes, I know. But it's been a long time. It's eleven years since I was here. And Chips was alive then."

"You worked with him, didn't you."

"Yes, for a year. I was in America when he died. Up in the Sonoma Valley in northern California. I was staying with some people I knew who had a vineyard. Phoebe's letter took a long time to find me, and I remember thinking then that if nobody ever told you that people you love have died, then they would live forever. And I thought then that I could never come back to Cornwall. But dying is part of life. I've learned that since. But I hadn't learned it then."

I thought of the carousel that Chips had made for me out of an old gramophone; he and Phoebe laughing together; the smell of his pipe.

"I loved him, too."

"Everybody did. He was such a benevolent man. I studied sculpture with him, but I learned from Chips a lot about living that, when you're twenty, is infinitely more important. I never knew my own father, and it always made me feel different towards other people. Chips filled that gap. He gave me a great sense of identity." I knew what he meant, because that was just the way I felt about Phoebe. "Coming down from London yesterday, I kept having second thoughts; wondering if I was doing the right thing. It isn't always wise to return to the place where you've been young and dreamed dreams. And had ambitions."

"Not if your dreams and ambitions came true. And surely that's happened for you. The Chastal exhibition must have proved that. There can't be a painting left unsold . . ."

"Perhaps I need to be unsure of myself."

"You can't have it all."

We fell silent. It was noon now, and the sun was very warm. I heard the soft buffet of the breeze, the lap of water against the seawall. Across the flooded estuary, from the distant causeway, came the hum of passing cars. A flock of gulls fought over a piece of rotting fish.

He said, "You know, once, centuries before

Christ, in the Bronze Age, this estuary was a river. Traders sailed all the way from the eastern Mediterranean, around the Lizard and Lands End, laden to the gunwales with all the treasures of the Levant."

I smiled. I said, "I've read *Vanishing Cornwall,* too."

"It's magic." He opened the book and it fell open at a much-studied page, and he read aloud:

For the watcher to-day, crouching amidst the sand dunes and the tufted grass, looking seaward to where the shallows run, imagination can take a riotous course, picturing line upon line of high-prowed, flat-bottomed craft, brightly coloured, their sails abeam, entering the river with the flood tide.

He closed the book. "I wish I had that sort of perception, but I haven't. I can only see the here and the now, and try to paint it the way it happens to me."

"Do you take that book everywhere with you?"

"No. But I found it in a shop in New York, and when I first read it I knew that someday, sometime, I had to come back to Cornwall. It never leaves you. It's like a magnet. You have to return."

"But why to the Castle Hotel, of all places?"

Daniel looked up at me, amused. "Why? Don't you think I fit in there?"

I thought of the rich Americans, the golfers, the twin-setted ladies playing bridge, the genteel teatime orchestra.

"Not exactly."

He laughed. "I know. It was a fairly incongruous choice, but it was the only hotel I could remember and I was tired. Jet-lag tired, London tired, everything tired. I wanted to get into an enormous bed and sleep for a week. And then when I woke up this morning, I wasn't tired any longer. And I thought about Chips and knew that all I wanted to do was come and see Phoebe again. So I walked down to the station and caught the train. And then got off the train and met you."

"And now," I told him, "you're coming back to the house with me, and you're going to stay for lunch. There's a bottle of wine in the fridge and Lily Tonkins has got a bit of lamb in the oven."

"Lily Tonkins? Is she still going?"

"She runs the house. She's doing all the cooking as well just now."

"I'd forgotten Lily." He picked up my sketch pad once more, and this time I didn't mind. He said, "You know, you're not only exceptionally pretty, but you are talented as well."

I decided to ignore the bit about being pretty. "I'm not talented. That's why I work for Marcus Bernstein. I found out the hard way that there was no hope of me earning a living by being an artist."

"How wise of you to realise," said Daniel Cassens. "So few people do."

Together, with the sun on our backs, we climbed the slope of the hill. I opened the wooden gate in the escallonia hedge, and he went ahead of me, cautiously, as a dog will go, nosing his way into once-familiar territory. I shut the gate. He stood looking up at the face of the house, and I looked, too, and tried to see it with his eyes, after eleven years away. To me, it looked as I had always know it. I saw the pointed Gothic windows, the garden door open to the brick terrace and the morning's warmth. There were still geraniums blooming in their earthenware tubs, and Phoebe's ramshackle garden chairs had not yet been put away for the winter.

We walked up the gentle slope of the lawn, and I led the way indoors.

"Phoebe?" I opened the kitchen door, from

whence came delicious smells of cooking lamb. Lily Tonkins was at the kitchen table, chopping mint, but she stopped when I appeared.

"She got home about five minutes ago. Went upstairs to change her shoes."

"I've brought a visitor for lunch. Is that all right?"

"Always plenty to eat. Friend of yours, is it?"

Daniel, behind me, moved into view. "It's me, Lily, Daniel Cassens."

Lily's mouth fell open. "Aw, my dear life." She laid down the chopping knife and put a hand to her meager chest, conveying heart-stopping shock. "The sight of you! Like a body out of the past. Daniel Cassens. It must be nearly twelve years. What are you doing here?"

"Come to see you," he told her. He walked around the table and stooped to kiss her cheek. Lily gave a crow of laughter and went pink. "You villain. Turning up like a bad penny. Just you wait till Miss Shackleton sets eyes on you. Us thought you'd forgotten all about we."

The Cornish frequently mix their pronouns, but Lily did this only under great stress, her voice shrill with excitement. "Did you know she'd broken her arm, poor soul? Been at the hospital all morning she has, but the doctor says she's doing nicely. Wait now, till I give her a shout." And she disappeared into the hall, and we heard her calling upstairs to Miss Shackleton to come down immediate, because there was some lovely surprise waiting for her.

Daniel followed her, but I stayed in the kitchen because for some reason I felt that if I witnessed their reunion I should probably burst into tears. As it was, it was Phoebe who cried. I'd never seen her cry before, but they were tears of joy and over in a moment. But still, she cried. And then we all found ourselves back in the kitchen, and I took the wine out of the refrigerator and Lily forgot about chopping mint and went to find some glasses, and the occasion then and there suddenly turned into a tremendous celebration.

He stayed for the rest of the afternoon. The day, which had started so brightly, became overcast, with low clouds blowing in from the sea on a rising wind. There were showers, and it became chilly, but none of this mattered, for we were indoors by the fire, and the hours flew by in talk and reminiscence and a general catching up on everything that had been happening to both of them.

I had little to add to the conversation, but that

did not matter. Listening was a joy, because not only did I feel that I was involved with both of them as people but because my interests and my work were relevant to everything that they discussed. I knew about this painter; I had heard of that exhibition; I had actually seen that particular portrait. Phoebe spoke of one Lewis Falcon, who was now living in a house out at Lanyon, and I remembered him because we had held an exhibition of his work at Marcus Bernstein's not two years before.

And we talked about Chips, and it was not like talking about a person who had died six years ago but as though at any moment he would walk into the firelit room to join us, sink into his own sagging armchair, join in the discussion.

Finally, they got onto the subject of Phoebe's own work. What was she doing now? Daniel wanted to know, and Phoebe laughed in her usual self-deprecating way and said that she had nothing to show him, but under pressure she admitted that there were a few canvases that she had completed last year, whilst on holiday in the Dordogne, but she had never got around to sorting them out and they were down in Chips's studio, still stacked haphazardly beneath dust sheets. Daniel at once sprang to his feet and insisted on seeing them, so Phoebe found the studio key and pulled on a raincoat and they set off together, down the brick path, to go and search them out.

I did not accompany them on this expedition. It was half past four and Lily Tonkins had gone home, so when I had collected our coffee mugs and washed them up, I laid a tea tray, found a fruitcake in a tin, and took the empty kettle off the Aga to fill it at the sink.

The sink in Phoebe's kitchen was beneath the window, which was pleasant, because it meant that while you were washing up, you could enjoy the view. But the view now was lost, drowned in a mistlike rain. The clouds were low, the wet, emptying sands of the estuary reflecting their leaden darkness. Flood tide, ebb tide. They made a pattern of time, like the minute hands of a clock, ticking life away.

I felt philosophic, peaceful. And then, suddenly, very happy. This happiness caught me unawares, as I used to be caught unawares by the random ecstasies of childhood. I looked around me, as though the source of this reasonless euphoria could be seen, pinned down, remembered. I saw everything in that familiar kitchen with a rare and heightened perception, so that each humble and ordinary object appeared both pleasing and beautiful. The grain of the scrubbed table, the bright colours of the crockery on the dresser, a basket of vegetables, the symmetry of cups and saucepans.

I thought about Daniel and Phoebe, rooting around together in Chips's dusty old studio. I was glad that I had not gone with them. I liked him. I liked his beautiful hands and his light, quick voice and dark eyes. But there was also something disturbing about him. I was not sure if I wanted to be disturbed.

He had said, "You are not only exceptionally pretty, but you are talented as well."

I was not used to being told I was pretty. My long straight hair was too pale, my mouth too big, my nose snub. Even Nigel Gordon, who—according to my mother—was in love with me, had never actually got around to saying that I was pretty. Smashing, maybe, or sensational, but never pretty. I wondered if Daniel was married and then laughed at myself, because my thought processes were so painfully obvious, and because it was exactly the question that my mother would have asked. My own self-ridicule broke the spell of that extraordinary moment of perception, and Phoebe's kitchen dissolved into its usual mundane self, left neat by Lily Tonkins before she had donned her head scarf and bicycled home to get her husband's tea.

When tea was over, Daniel pushed back his cuff, looked at his watch, and said that he must go.

"I wish you were staying here," said Phoebe. "Why can't you come back here? Fetch your things and then come back to us."

But he said that he wouldn't. "Lily Tonkins has got quite enough on her plate looking after the pair of you."

"But we'll see you again? You're down for a little?"

He stood up. "A day or two, anyway." It sounded vague. "I'll be back to see you."

"How are you going to get back to Porthker-ris?"

"There's probably a bus . . ."

I said, "I'll drive you in Phoebe's car. It's a mile to the bus stop and it's still raining and you'll get soaked."

"Don't you mind?"

"Of course I don't mind."

So he said good-bye to Phoebe and we went out and got into her battered old car, and I backed it cautiously out of the garage and we drove off, leaving Phoebe silhouetted in the lighted doorway of Holly Cottage, waving her good arm and wishing us a safe journey, as though we were setting off on some marathon rally.

We bowled up the hill through the rain, past the golf club, onto the main road. "You're so clever to drive," he said admiringly.

"But you can surely drive a car. Everybody can drive a car."

"Yes, I can drive, but I simply hate it. I'm a total fool about anything mechanical."

"Have you never had a car?"

"I had to have one in America. Everybody has a car in America. But I never really felt at home with it. I bought it secondhand, and it was enormous, long as a bus, with a radiator like a mouth organ and huge, phallic headlights and exhaust pipes. It had automatic gears, too, and electrically operated windows, and some sort of supercharged carburetor. I was terrified of it. When I'd had it three years, I finally sold it, but by that time I'd only just worked out how to operate the heater."

I began to laugh. I suddenly thought of Phoebe saying, when you settle down with a man, it is absolutely vital that he makes you laugh. Nigel, it was true, had never made me laugh much. On the other hand, he was a wizard with cars, and spent a good deal of his spare time either with his head under the hood of his M.G., or else prone beneath it, with only his feet sticking out, and conversation reduced to requests for a larger monkey wrench.

I said, comfortingly, "You can't be good at everything. If you're a successful artist, it would be too much to ask to be a mechanic as well."

"That's what's so fantastic about Phoebe. She paints like a dream. She could have made a really great name for herself if she hadn't happily subjugated her talent in creating a home for Chips . . . and for all the stray students like myself who lived with them and worked with them and learned so much from them. Holly Cottage was a sort of refuge for so many young and struggling artists. There were always immense, delicious meals, and order and cleanliness and warmth. You never forget that sort of security and comfort. It instills in you a standard of good living—and I mean 'good' in the true sense of the word—for the rest of your life."

It was marvellously satisfying to hear another person state aloud what I had always felt myself about Phoebe, and yet, somehow, had never been able to express.

I said, "We're the same, you and I. When I was a child, it was just about the only time I ever cried, when I had to say good-bye to Phoebe, and get on the train and go back to London. And yet once I was home again, back with my mother, and with my own room, and all my own things around me, it was all right. And by the next day, I was always quite happy again, and involved, and glued to the telephone, ringing up all my friends."

"The tears would have been the direct result of the insecurity of two different worlds touching. Nothing makes one more miserable."

I thought about this. It made sense. I said, "I suppose so."

"Actually, I can't imagine you being anything but a happy little girl."

"Yes, I was happy. My parents were divorced, but they were both wise and intelligent people. And it all happened when I was very little, so that it didn't leave what you might call a lasting scar."

"You were lucky."

"Yes, I was. I was always loved and I was always wanted. You can't ask more than that out of any childhood."

Now the road sloped and curved towards Porthkerris. Through the murk, the lights of the harbour sparkled far below us. We came to the gates of the Castle Hotel, and turned in, and made our way up the winding drive, the avenue of oak trees. There was an open space, with tennis courts and putting greens, and then a wide gravel sweep in front of the hotel. Lights shone from windows and the glassed revolving door. I drew up between a Porsche and a Jaguar, pulled on the brake and turned off the engine.

"I can't help feeling very slightly out of place. Do you know, I've never been here before. Nobody's ever been rich enough to bring me."

"Come in and I'll buy you a drink."

"I'm not suitably dressed."

"Neither am I." He opened the door. "Come on."

We left the car, looking dusty and forlorn between its aristocratic neighbors, and Daniel led the way through the revolving doors, and inside it was tremendously warm and thickly carpeted and expensive-smelling. It was that slack period between tea and cocktail time, and there were not many people about; only a man in golf clothes, reading the *Financial Times*, and an elderly couple watching television.

The hall porter gave us a cold glance, then recognised Daniel and hastily rearranged his expression.

"Good evening, sir."

"Good evening," said Daniel and headed straight in the direction of the bar. But it was my first visit to the Castle, and I wanted to linger and inspect. Here was a writing room, and here, visible through open double doors, an overheated, overupholstered apartment arranged as a card room. In this, by a blazing fire, sat four ladies around a bridge table. I paused for a moment, my attention caught; the scene was so reminiscent of some play from the thirties. I felt that somewhere I had seen it all before: the long brocade curtains, the chintz-covered chairs, the set piece of the elaborate flower arrangement.

Even the ladies wore the correct clothes: the cashmere cardigans, the strings of good pearls. One smoked a cigarette with a long ivory holder.

"Two no trumps."

"Prue." Daniel, impatient, had retraced his steps to urge me on. "Come *on.*"

I was about to follow him when the lady who faced me across the card table looked up. Our eyes met. I had not instantly recognised her, but now I was face to face with Mrs. Tolliver.

"Prue." She looked politely pleased to see me, though I found it hard to believe that this was so. "What a surprise."

"Hello, Mrs. Tolliver."

"What are you doing here?"

I did not want to go and talk to them, but confronted by the situation, I couldn't think of anything else to do. "I . . . I was just looking around. I've never been here before." I moved forward into the room, and the other ladies looked up at me from their hands of cards with smiling mouths and eyes that did not miss a detail of my windblown hair, my old pullover, my faded jeans.

Mrs. Tolliver laid down her cards and introduced me to her friends. ". . . Prue Shackleton. You must know Phoebe Shackleton, who lives at Penmarron. Well, Prue is her niece . . ."

"Oh, yes. How nice," said the ladies in their various ways, obviously longing to get on with their game.

"Prue was so kind to Charlotte yesterday. She travelled down with her from London on the train."

The ladies smiled again, approving of this. I realised with some dismay that I had not thought of Charlotte all day. For some reason this made me feel guilty, and the guilt was not assuaged by the sight of Mrs. Tolliver sitting here in her element and playing bridge.

I said, "Where is Charlotte?"

"At home. With Mrs. Curnow."

"Is she all right?"

Mrs. Tolliver fixed me with a cold eye. "Is there any reason she shouldn't be?"

I was taken aback. "No reason . . ." I met her eye. "It's just that, on the train, she seemed very quiet."

"She's always quiet. She never has much to say. And how did you find Phoebe? Not bothered by her broken arm? I'm so glad. Is she with you now?"

"No. I just drove someone back . . . he's staying here . . ."

I remembered Daniel then, standing behind me, and in some confusion turned to include him in this little encounter and introduce him to Mrs. Tolliver.

"Daniel, this is Mrs . . ."

But he wasn't behind me. I saw only the open doors and the empty foyer beyond.

"Your friend took one look at us and left," one of the other ladies remarked, and I turned back and saw them laughing as though it were a joke. I smiled too.

"How silly of me. I thought he was still there."

Mrs. Tolliver picked up her cards once more

and arranged them in a neat fan. "So nice to have seen you," she said. I found myself, for no reason, blushing. I made my excuses, said good-bye to them, and left.

Back in the foyer, I searched for Daniel. There was no trace of him, but I saw the lighted sign of the Cocktail Bar and headed for it, and found him, a solitary figure, sitting on a high stool with his back to me.

I was indignant. "What did you go off like that for?"

"Bridge-playing ladies aren't really my scene."

"They aren't my scene either, but sometimes you have to talk to people. I felt such a fool. I was going to introduce you and you'd evaporated into thin air. It was Mrs. Tolliver, from Penmarron."

"I know. Have a drink."

"If you knew it was Mrs. Tolliver, that was even ruder."

"You sound like an etiquette writer. Why should I be bothered with Mrs. Tolliver? No, don't tell me, because I don't want to know. Now I'm having a Scotch. What do you want to drink?"

"I don't know if I want a drink." I was still feeling put out.

"I thought that having a drink was what we'd come to do."

"Oh, all right." I climbed up onto the stool beside him. "I'll have a lager."

He ordered it for me. We then proceeded to sit in silence. At the back of the bar the shelves of bottles were backed by mirrored glass, and our two reflections gazed back at us from behind them. Daniel took out a cigar and lit it, and the barman brought me my lager and made a few remarks about the weather. He gave us a dish of peanuts. When he had gone back to the other end of the long bar, Daniel said, "All right, I'm sorry."

"What for?"

"For insulting Mrs. Tolliver, and for being bloody to you. I am in fact quite often bloody. It's as well to know before we embark on some deathless friendship." He looked at me and smiled.

"You didn't insult her." I added ruefully, "To be perfectly truthful, I don't much like her either."

"How do you come to be on such intimate terms with her?"

"Talking to someone at a bridge table isn't exactly being intimate."

"But you do know her quite well?"

"No, I don't. But my mother used to play bridge with her when we came down to stay with Phoebe. And then yesterday I travelled down on the train from London with her little granddaughter, Charlotte Collis. Her mother is Annabelle Tolliver. She was sitting next to me and she looked rather miserable, so we went and had lunch together. There was . . ." I decided not to go into the details of Charlotte's predicament, ". . . some complication, and she can't be at her boarding school, so she's spending a week with Mrs. Tolliver. Phoebe says she's a lonely child; she's always at Holly Cottage, just to have someone to talk to."

Daniel, quietly smoking his cigar, said nothing. I wondered if I was boring him stiff and looked to see if he was politely stifling yawns. But he wasn't. He was simply sitting, his elbow propped on the bar, his profile showing no expression, his eyes downcast. The smoke of his cigar made a fragrant, curling plume.

I took a mouthful of delicious icy lager. "Mrs. Tolliver didn't really want her to stay, according to Phoebe. She didn't even come to the junction to meet Charlotte off the train, and Charlotte and I had to share Mr. Thomas's taxi. And now, today, Mrs. Tolliver's playing bridge, and she's left the child with her housekeeper. It can't be much fun for Charlotte. She's only about ten. She should be with other children."

After a little, Daniel said, "Yes." He put out his half-smoked cigar, grinding the stub into the ashtray as though he had a grudge against it. He finished his drink and set down the empty glass, then turned and smiled at me and said, surprisingly, "Tomorrow. Will you come and have lunch with me?"

Taken unawares, I did not immediately reply. He went on, swiftly, "That is, if Phoebe can spare you. And lend you her car again."

"I think she could. I don't think she'd mind."

"Ask her, then, when you get back."

"All right. Shall I come here? To the hotel?"

"No. I'll meet you in the Ship Inn on the harbour in Porthkerris. We'll get a ploughman's lunch and a glass of beer, and if it's fine we'll go and sit on the harbour wall and pretend we're tourists."

I smiled. "What time?"

He shrugged. "About half past twelve."

"All right." I was very pleased that he had asked me. "Half past twelve."

He said, "Good. Now finish your lager and I'll take you back to the car."

* * *

We emerged from the revolving doors, ejected into wet darkness. We found Phoebe's car, and Daniel opened the door for me, but before I could get into it, he had put his hand around the back of my neck and drawn my face towards his and kissed my mouth. His face was damp with the rain, and for an instant we stood there, and I felt the cool pressure of his cheek against my own.

We said good night. I drove giddily back to Penmarron, feeling drunk, as though I had consumed a great deal more than a single half-pint of lager.

I was bursting to tell Phoebe about everything and to indulge in more long and illuminating discussions about Daniel and Mrs. Tolliver and Charlotte, but when I got back to Hólly Cottage, I disturbed her dozing by the fire, and when she woke up, she admitted that she was very tired. Her arm ached, the cast was heavy, the day had been long and exciting. She looked tired, too, her face, beneath the obliterating brim of her hat, thin and shadowed. So I told her only that Daniel had asked me to have lunch with him the next day and asked if this would be all right and if I could borrow her car. She was, as I had known she would be, perfectly agreeable, so I went off to the kitchen and poured her a glass of restoring wine, and then I made scrambled eggs and we ate them in front of the fire.

After that, although it was only half past eight, she decided that she would go to bed, so I helped her upstairs and switched on the electric blanket and drew the curtains against the chilly darkness. When I left her, cozy in her huge bed, she was reading a book by the light of the bedside lamp, but as I shut the door and took myself downstairs, I knew that very soon she would be asleep.

Chapter 4

NEXT MORNING I was out of bed before she could be, and downstairs. It was too early for Lily Tonkins, so I laid a tray for Phoebe's breakfast, made coffee and toast, and carried the lot upstairs. She was already awake, watching through her open window the sun climb the sky. When I appeared through the door, she turned her head on the pillow and saw the tray and said, with all her usual energy, "You are an idiot, Prue; you know I never have breakfast in bed."

"You are this morning." She pulled herself up on her pillows, and I laid the tray across her knees and went to close the window.

"Red sky at morning, shepherd's warning. I suppose it's going to rain today."

"Don't be so gloomy. You haven't brought a coffee cup for yourself."

"I thought you'd like to be left in peace."

"I hate being left in peace. I like chatting over breakfast. Go and get a mug." She took the lid off the coffee pot and peered inside. "You've made enough for ten people; you'll have to help me drink it."

In bed, which was about the only place she did not wear one of her dashing hats, she looked different: feminine; older, perhaps; vulnerable. Her thick, wiry hair hung in a plait over one shoulder, and she was wrapped in a fleecy shawl. She looked so comfortable that I said, "Why don't you stay there for the morning? Lily Tonkins can cope with everything, and there's not much that you can do to help with only one arm."

"I might," said Phoebe, not committing herself. "I just might do that. Now go and get a mug before the coffee gets cold."

I fetched not only a cup but a bowl of cereal as well, and ate it sitting on the edge of the great, carved pine bed that Phoebe and Chips had shared for all those happy, sinful years. She had once told me that everything she really enjoyed in life was either illegal, immoral, or fattening, and then had roared with laughter.

But somehow they had got away with it, she and Chips. Even in this small, parochial village, they had ridden out the inevitable storm of prejudice by sheer strength of character coupled with their disarming charm. I remembered Chips playing the organ in church when the regular organist had flu, and Phoebe busily baking enormous, lopsided cakes for the Women's Institute tea.

She cared for everybody, and yet for no person's opinion. I looked at her eating toast and marmalade and loved her. She caught my eye. She said, "How nice that you're having lunch with Daniel. What time are you meeting him?"

"Half past twelve at the Ship Inn in Porthkerris. But I won't go unless you promise me that you'll be all right."

"For heaven's sake, I'm not in a wheelchair. Off you go. But I shall want to hear all about it when you get back. Blow-by-blow descriptions." Her eyes twinkled, her cheeks bunched up in wicked laughter, and she was so obviously back to her normal good spirits that I started to tell her about the previous evening and our encounter with Mrs. Tolliver.

". . . And it was very embarrassing, because I

thought Daniel was just behind me, and I said something stupid like, 'I want you to meet my friend,' and when I turned round, he wasn't there. Disappeared. Bolted to the bar."

"Did Mrs. Tolliver see him?"

"I've no idea." I thought about this. "Does it make any difference?"

"No-o-o . . ." said Phoebe.

I frowned at her. "Phoebe, you're holding something back."

She laid down her coffee cup and gazed abstractedly out the window. After a bit she shrugged and said, "Oh, well, I don't suppose it matters talking about it now. It all happened so long ago, anyway. Water under the bridge. And it wasn't anything very desperate even then."

"What wasn't desperate?"

"Well . . . when Daniel was living with us, when he was a very young man, Annabelle Tolliver came down from London to spend the summer with her mother, and . . . well . . . I suppose you could say that they had a little fling. A flingette," she added hopefully, trying to make it sound trivial.

Daniel and Annabelle Tolliver. I stared at Phoebe. "You mean, he fancied Annabelle."

" 'Fancied.' " She chuckled. "Such a lovely old-fashioned word. Like 'frock.' Nobody wears frocks anymore." She gave a sigh and got back to the point. "No. Not exactly. If truth be told, I think it was Annabelle who fancied Daniel."

"But she must have been much older than he was."

"Oh, certainly. At least eight years."

"And married."

"Yes, married, too. But I told you, that never made much difference to Annabelle. She had a child by that time. Michael. He must have been about four years old. Poor child, even then I remember, he looked exactly like his father!"

"But . . ." Phoebe's endless digressions did nothing to clarify the situation. "What *happened?*"

"Oh, heavens, nothing happened. They used to go to parties together, picnics on the beach, swimming. She had a very flashy car that summer. It had a hood you could put down, and they used to drive all over the place together; very dashing they looked, too. Very eye-catching. Oh, you can imagine it, Prue."

I could. Only too clearly. "But I wouldn't have thought that Daniel . . ." I stopped, because I wasn't sure what I did think.

"You wouldn't have thought that Daniel was the social type. Perhaps he wasn't, but he was a very attractive young man. Still is, for that matter. And it must have flattered his ego to have her so eager to spend her time with him. I told you, she was beautiful. There were always queues of men swooning around her like lovesick cows. Or do I mean lovesick bulls? But Daniel was always a very quiet person. I think it was his quietness that intrigued Annabelle."

"How long did this go on?"

"The whole summer, on and off. It was just a little flirtation. Perfectly harmless."

"What did Mrs. Tolliver have to say about it?"

"Mrs. Tolliver never says anything about anything. She's the sort of woman who truly believes that if you don't look, it will go away. Besides, she must have realised that if it wasn't Daniel, it would have been some other man. Perhaps she reckoned that he was the lesser of a lot of other evils."

"But the little boy . . . Michael?"

"There was a starchy nanny taking care of him. He never got in the way at all."

"And her husband . . ." I could hardly bear to say his horrid name. "Leslie Collis?"

"He was left in London, running his office. I suppose living in some service flat or other. I've no idea. It's not important, anyway."

I thought carefully through this extraordinary revelation. I finally said, "Then last night . . . you think that's why Daniel didn't want to talk to Mrs. Tolliver."

"Maybe. Maybe he just didn't want to get involved with four bridge-playing ladies."

"I wonder why he didn't tell me himself."

"There was no reason he should. It has nothing to do with you, and it was a total nonevent, anyway." She poured herself more coffee and said, quite briskly, "You're not to make anything of it."

"I'm not. I just wish it had been anybody but Annabelle Tolliver."

Red sky at morning, shepherd's warning. But it was the sort of day when you couldn't be sure what would happen to the weather. A warm, west-wind sort of day, with gusts that tore leaves from trees and sent them flying and flecked the indigo sea with white horses. The sky was a brazen blue swept by high clouds, and the very air seemed to glitter. From the top of the hill above Porthkerris, I could see for miles, long beyond the lighthouse to the distant spur of Trevose Head. From the harbour far below me, a solitary fishing boat butted out into the choppy sea, making for the deep water beneath the cliffs of Lanyon.

The way led steeply downhill, through the narrow streets of the little town. Most of the summer visitors had now departed. Only a handful, looking chilly in shorts, stood about outside the news agent's or made their way down the hill to where a bakery was redolent with the smell of fresh, hot pastries.

At Porthkerris the Ship Inn stands, where it has stood for three hundred years or more, on the harbour road by the old quay where the fishermen used to land their pilchards. I drove by it, but there was no sign of Daniel, so I found a place to park the Volkswagen and then walked back along the cobbles and went in, dipping my head beneath the low, smoke-blackened lintel. Inside, after the brightness of the day, it was very dark. A small coal fire burned in the grate, and an old man sat by this, looking as though he had sat there all his life or had, perhaps, grown up out of the floorboards.

"Prue."

I turned. Daniel was sitting in the deep window seat with an empty pint tankard on a wobbly table that had been made out of a barrel. He stood up, easing himself from behind this table, and said, "It's too good a day to have lunch indoors. What do you think?"

"So what shall we do?"

"Buy something. Eat it on the beach."

So we went out again and down the road until we reached one of those convenient shops that seem to sell everything. We bought fresh pastries, so hot that the man had to wrap them in newspaper. We bought a bag of apples, and some chocolate biscuits, and a packet of paper cups, and a bottle of dubious red wine. When the kindly man realised we were going to drink it right away, he threw in a corkscrew as well.

We went back out into the sunshine and crossed the cobbled street, and climbed down the stone steps that were dry at the top and coated with green weed at the bottom. The tide was on its way out and had left behind it a sickle of clean yellow sand. There was a cluster of rocks pounded smooth by the seas of centuries, and we settled ourselves on these, sheltered from the wind and with the sun on our faces. Screaming gulls wheeled in the windy air, and from where some men worked peacefully on a boat came the pleasant sounds of hammer blows and muted voices.

Daniel opened the bottle of wine, and we unwrapped the pastries. I was suddenly very hungry. I bit greedily into mine, and it was so hot that I nearly scalded my mouth and bits of steaming potato fell out of the pastry onto the sand, to be spied and scooped up in an instant by a great, greedy gull.

I said, "This was a brilliant idea."

"I have them, every now and again."

And I thought that if it had been Nigel, we would in all probability have been lunching at the Castle Hotel, with white tablecloths and waiters hovering, hampering conversation. Daniel had taken the cork out of the bottle; now he took a mouthful of wine, considered its taste, and swallowed it.

"An amusing and unpretentious little wine," he said, "if you don't mind it being stone cold. I don't suppose it improves its bouquet, drinking it out of a paper cup, but beggars can't be choosers. The only alternative seems to be the neck of the bottle." He took a bite out of his pastry. "How's Phoebe this morning?"

"She was tired last night. She went to bed early, and this morning I took her up her breakfast in bed, and she promised she'd stay there till lunchtime."

"What would she have done if you hadn't been able to come to Penmarron and take care of her?"

"She'd have managed. Lily would have looked

after her, but Lily can't drive, and Phoebe hates being without her car."

"Were you able to get away from work just like that? What does Marcus Bernstein do without you?"

"I was on holiday anyway for two weeks, so that was no problem. He'd already engaged a temp to take over while I was away."

"You mean you had two weeks' holiday and you weren't going to do anything with it? What were you going to do, stay in London?"

"No. As a matter of fact, I was meant to be going to Scotland."

"Scotland? For heaven's sake, what were you going to do there?"

"Stay with people."

"Have you ever been to Scotland?"

"No. Have you?"

"Once. Everybody kept telling me how beautiful it was, but it rained so hard that I never found out if they were telling the truth or not." He took another mouthful of pastry. "Who were you going to stay with?"

"Friends."

"You're being cagey, aren't you? You might as well tell me all, because I'll just go on asking questions until you give me some answers. It's a boy-friend, isn't it?"

I would not look at him. "Why should it be?"

"Because you're far too attractive not to have some man languishing with love for you. And you've got the most extraordinary expression on your face. Confused nonchalance."

"I'm sure that's a contradiction of terms."

"What's he called?"

"Who?"

"Oh, stop being coy. The boyfriend, of course."

"Nigel Gordon."

"Nigel. Nigel's one of my most unfavorite names."

"It's no worse than Daniel."

"It's a wet name. Timothy's a wet name, too. So is Jeremy. And Christopher. And Nicholas."

"Nigel is not wet."

"What is he, then?"

"Nice."

"What does he do?"

"He's an insurance broker."

"And he comes from Scotland?"

"Yes. His family lives there. In Inverness-shire."

"What a frightfully good thing you didn't go. You'd have hated it. A great unheated house, with bedrooms cold as refrigerators and baths encased in mahogany, like coffins."

I said, "Daniel, you make more ridiculous sweeping statements than any man I've ever met."

"You won't marry him, will you, this Highland insurance broker? Please don't. I can't bear the thought of you in kilts and living in Inverness-shire."

I very nearly laughed but managed to keep a prim face. "I wouldn't be living in Inverness-shire. I'd be living in Nigel's desirable residence in South Kensington." I threw what remained of my pastry to the gulls and helped myself to an apple, rubbing it to a shine on the sleeve of my sweater. "And I wouldn't have to work, either. I wouldn't have to go trudging off to Marcus Bernstein's every morning. I could be a lady of leisure, with time to do all I want to do, which is paint. And it wouldn't matter if nobody bought my pictures, because my husband would be there, ready and willing to pay all the bills."

He said, "I thought you thought like Phoebe. I'm disillusioned."

"Perhaps sometimes I think like my mother. She likes life to be neat and squared off and conventional and safe. She adores Nigel. She's longing for me to marry him. She can't wait to start planning a wedding. St. Paul's, Knightsbridge, and a reception in Pavilion Road . . ."

"And a honeymoon at Budleigh Salterton, with the golf clubs in the boot of the car. Prue, you can't be serious."

I took a great bite of the shiny apple. "I might be."

"Not about a man called Nigel."

I was beginning to feel irritated. "You know nothing about him. And anyway, what's so bad about getting married? You think the world of Phoebe, you thought the world of Chips. But, you know, they would have been married, years ago, if only Chips could have gotten a divorce. But he couldn't. So they compromised, and made the very best of their life together."

"I don't think there's anything wrong in getting married. I just think it's insane to get married to the wrong person."

"I suppose you've never made that mistake."

"No, as a matter of fact, I haven't. I've done just about everything else. Made every other sort of mistake, but getting married wasn't one of them." He appeared to be considering this state of affairs. "Never even thought about it, as a matter of fact."

He smiled at me, and I smiled back, because for

no particular reason I was filled with gladness, simply because he had never married. And yet I was not surprised. There was something nomadic, free, about Daniel, and I found I was envious of this.

I said, "I wish there was time in life to do everything."

"You've got time."

"I know, but already I seem to be in a sort of rut. I like the rut. I like my job and I'm doing exactly what I want to do, and I love Marcus Bernstein, and I wouldn't change my job for anything in the world. But sometimes, on a certain sort of morning, I drive to work, and I think, I'm twenty-three and what am I doing with my life? And I think of all the places I long to see. Kashmir and the Bahamas and Greece, and Palmyra. And San Francisco, and Peking and Japan. I would like to have been to some of the places you've been to."

"Then go. Go now."

"You make it sound so simple."

"It can be. Life is as simple as you make it."

"Perhaps I haven't got that sort of courage. But still, I would like to have done some of the things you've done."

He laughed. "Don't wish that. Some of it was hell."

"It can't still be hell. Everything's going so well for you now."

"Uncertainty is always hell."

"What are you uncertain about?"

"About what I'm going to do next."

"That shouldn't be too frightening."

"I'm thirty-one. Within the next twelve months I've got to make some sort of a decision; I'm frightened of drifting. I don't want to drift for the rest of my life."

"What do you want to do?"

"I want . . ."

He leaned back against the knobby granite of the harbour wall and turned his face to the sun and closed his eyes. He looked like a man who longed for the oblivion of sleep. "When this exhibition at Peter Chastal's is over and finished with, I want to go to Greece. There's an island called Spetsai, and on Spetsai there is a house, square and white as a sugar cube. And there's a terrace with terra cotta tiles on the floor, and geraniums in pots along the tops of the wall. And below the terrace there's a mooring and a boat with a white sail like the wing of a gull. Not a big boat. Just large enough for two." I waited. He opened his eyes. He said, "I think I shall go there."

"Do that thing."

"Would you come?" He held out his hand to me. "Would you like to come and visit me? You just told me you wanted to go to Greece. Would you come and let me show you some of its glories?"

I was very touched. I laid my hand in his and felt his fingers close about my wrist. How different this was, how frighteningly different, from the invitation Nigel had painfully offered me, to visit his mother in Inverness-shire. Two different worlds. *The insecurity of two different worlds touching.* I wondered if I was about to burst into tears.

"One day," I told him, in the voice of a mother placating an insistent child. "One day, maybe, I'll be able to come."

The sky clouded and it grew cold. It was time to stir ourselves. We gathered up the picnic rubbish and found a little bin by a lamp post, and threw all the trash into that. We walked back to where I had left Phoebe's car, and there was the smell of rain in the air and the sea had turned angry and leaden.

Red sky at morning, shepherd's warning. We got into the car and slowly drove back to Penmarron. Phoebe's heater did not work, and I felt cold. I knew that there would be a fire ablaze at Holly Cottage, and possibly crumpets for tea, but I wasn't thinking about these things. My mind was filled with images of Greece, of the house above the water and the boat with a sail like the wing of a gull. I thought of swimming in that dark Aegean sea, the water warm and clear as glass . . .

Memory stirred.

"Daniel."

"What is it?"

"That night I got off the train from London, I had a dream. It was about swimming. I was on a desert island, and I had to walk a long long way through shallow water. And then all at once it was deep, but so clear I could see right to the bottom. And once I had started to swim, there was a current. Very fast and strong. It was like being swept down a river."

I remembered again the sensation of peace, of blissful acceptance.

"What happened then?"

"Nothing. But it was nice."

"Sounds a good dream. What brought it to mind?"

"I was thinking about Greece. Swimming in Homer's wine-dark seas."

"All dreams have meaning."

"I know."

"What do you think that one signified?"

I told him, "I thought perhaps it was about dying."

But that was before Daniel had come into my life. Now I was wiser, and I knew that the dream was not about dying at all but loving.

When we got back to Holly Cottage, there was no sign of Phoebe. The firelit sitting room was empty, and when I called up the stair, thinking that perhaps she had spent the whole day in her bed, there was no reply.

But sounds of clashing crockery and opening drawers came from the kitchen. I went down the hall with Daniel behind me to open the door and investigate, only to discover Lily Tonkins engaged in whisking up a bowl of batter.

"You're back then," she said. She did not look too pleased to see us, and I wondered if she was in one of her cross moods. Lily could get very cross. Not with us in particular but just with the world in general, which included her morose husband, the cheeky girl who worked in the grocer's, and the man in the town hall who dealt with Lily's pension.

"Where's Phoebe?" I asked.

Lily did not look up from her task. "Gone down to the water."

"I hoped she'd stay in bed today."

"Stay in bed?" Lily set down the bowl with a thump and faced me with her arms akimbo. "Some chance she's had of staying in bed. We've had that little Charlotte Collis here all day, ever since ten o'clock this morning. I'd just taken Miss Shackleton a nice cup of tea and was polishing up the brasses when I heard a ring at the bell. Dratted nuisance, I said to myself, and went to the door, and there she was. And been here ever since."

"Where's Mrs. Tolliver?"

"Gone over to Falmouth for some meeting— Save the Children or Save the Church or something. Seems funny to me. I mean, I can understand some people don't like looking after children. There are some that do and some that don't. But she's that little girl's granny. No business to be up and about all the time, playing cards and saving things. Somebody's got to look after the little girl."

"Where's Mrs. Curnow?"

"Betty Curnow, she's there all right, up at White Lodge, but she's got her own work to do. Mrs. Tolliver can't be bothered to look after the child, then she should pay some other person to do the job."

"So what happened?"

"Well, I let her in, poor little soul, and I said Miss Shackleton was still in bed and you were out, gone for lunch. So she went up the stairs to see Miss Shackleton, and I heard them talking together. Talk, talk, you'd think that child had never had a soul to talk to the way she carries on when she's here. Then she came down, the little girl, and said Miss Shackleton was getting up and getting dressed. And that vexed me because I knew she needed a good rest. So I went up and gave her a hand with her clothes, and then down she came and phoned Betty Curnow and said that we were keeping Charlotte here and giving her lunch. Luckily there was a bit of cold lamb, and I peeled a few potatoes and made a custard, but it's not right Miss Shackleton being landed with the child to take care of, and her with that bad arm and everything."

I had never seen Lily so loquacious or upset. She was concerned, and naturally so, for Phoebe. But, as well, she had a kind heart. The Cornish love children, and Lily was no exception. She had decided that Charlotte was being neglected, and all her hackles were well and truly up.

I said, "I'm sorry. I should have been here to help you."

Daniel had listened to all this in silence. Now he said, "Where are they?"

"Went down to the shore to do their drawing. That's what they like to do when they're together, like a pair of old women." She turned from the table and went to the sink to peer out the window. Daniel and I followed her. We saw the empty estuary, the deserted sands. But at the far end of the seawall we could discern the two distant figures: Phoebe, unmistakable in her hat, and the child beside her, wearing a scarlet anorak. They had taken camp stools with them and sat side by side, very close. There was something touching about the pair of them. Oblivious to the rest of the world, they looked as though they had been washed up by some unimaginable storm and forgotten.

As we stood there, there came the first sharp rattle of raindrops against the glass of the window, and Lily said, "There now!" as if she had forecast this very thing happening. "That's the dratted rain come on. And Miss Shackleton won't even notice. Once she starts her sketching, that's the end of it. Might as well shout your heart out, and she'd never take notice. And her with that cast on her arm, poor soul . . ."

The time had obviously come to intervene. "I'll go and get them," I said.

"No." Daniel laid a restraining hand on my arm. "It's pouring. I'll go."

"You'll need a mackintosh, Daniel," Lily warned him, but he found an umbrella in the hall and set off armed with that. I watched his progress, the umbrella held high over his head, as he walked down across the lawn and disappeared through the gate in the escallonia hedge. Moments later he came into view once more, making his way along the edge of the seawall towards the two unsuspecting artists.

Lily and I turned away from the window. "What can I do to help you?" I asked.

"You could lay the table for tea."

"Let's all have it in here. It's so nice and warm."

"I'm making a batch of pancakes." She picked up her bowl and started whisking again. She looked more cheerful, having aired her grievances, and I was grateful for this.

I said, "Tomorrow I'll do something with Charlotte. Take her somewhere in the car, perhaps. She's been on my conscience ever since I arrived, only there doesn't seem to have been much time to arrange anything."

"Mind, she's a nice enough little girl."

"I know. But somehow that only makes it worse."

The table was laid, the drop scones made, and the kettle boiling, and still they had not returned.

"That Daniel," observed Lily. "He's as bad as the rest of them. Probably forgot what he went for, and he's sat down with them to paint a picture for himself . . ."

"I'd better go." I found an old raincoat of Phoebe's and a man-eating sou'wester that had once belonged to Chips and let myself out the garden door. It was now raining hard and very wet, but as I crossed the grass Daniel and Phoebe appeared at the gate, Daniel holding the camp stools under one arm and the umbrella high over Phoebe's head with the other. Phoebe, except for her hat, was dressed as though for a sunny outing, and her cardigan, buttoned bulkily over her plaster cast, was sodden, her shoes and stout stockings mud-splashed. She carried in her good hand her painting bag, a sturdy and familiar piece of equipment made of canvas, and as Daniel opened the gate for her, she looked up and saw me.

"Hello! Here we are, a lot of drowned rats!"

"Lily and I wondered what had happened to you all."

"Charlotte hadn't quite finished, and she wanted to."

"Where is she?"

"Oh, coming. Somewhere," said Phoebe, airily.

I looked past her, down the hill, and saw Charlotte at the foot of it. She stood with her back to me, peering into the depths of a dripping bramble bush.

I said, resigned, "I'd better get her," and set off down the wet and slippery slope. "Charlotte! Come along."

She turned and looked up and saw me. Her hair clung to her head, and her glasses were misted with rain.

"What *are* you doing?"

"I'm looking for blackberries. I thought there might be some."

"You're not meant to be looking for blackberries, you're meant to be coming up to the house for tea. Lily's made pancakes."

She moved reluctantly. "All right." Even the lure of hot pancakes did not kindle much enthusiasm. I thought that it would be easy to be maddened by her, and yet I understood her reluctance to end an afternoon spent in Phoebe's delightful company. I remembered myself at Charlotte's age, trailing home after a day with Phoebe, spent perhaps on the beach or picking primroses or riding in the little train to Porthkerris. It had always been an effort to drag oneself back to routine, and meals, and everyday, mundane life.

I held out my hand to her. "Do you want a pull up the hill?"

She took her hand out of her anorak pocket and gave it to me. It felt thin and small and wet and cold. I said, "What you need is a good rub-down with a towel and a hot drink." We set off up the slope. "Did you have a good afternoon with Phoebe?"

"Yes. We've been drawing."

"I don't suppose you even noticed the rain."

"No, not really. My paper was beginning to get a bit wet, but then that man came and held the umbrella over it and I could finish."

"His name is Daniel."

"I know. Phoebe's told me about him. He used to live with her and Chips."

"He's a famous artist now."

"I know that, too. He said my drawing was very good."

"What did you draw?"

"I tried to draw some gulls, but they kept flying away, so I did a made-up picture."

"That was enterprising."

"He said it was very good."

"I hope you haven't left it behind?"

"No. Phoebe put it in her bag."

Breathless by now, we toiled on in silence. We reached the gate. I opened it, and as Charlotte went through, I said, "I've been wondering how you've been getting along. I would have rung you up or asked you to tea, only I've been so . . ." I hesitated, searching for the right word. "Busy" seemed scarcely truthful.

"It's not much fun," said Charlotte with a child's uncompromising honesty.

I made a cheerful face. "Well, perhaps tomorrow we could do something together." I shut the gate behind us. "Go somewhere in the car if Phoebe doesn't need it."

Charlotte considered this. Then, "Do you think," she said, "that Daniel would like to come too?"

As soon as we were inside the kitchen, Lily, half-irritated and half-laughing, pounced on Charlotte, unzipping her drenched jacket, kneeling to struggle with the buckles of her sandals.

"I don't know, some people can be that silly. Miss Shackleton, well, I've never seen a soul so wet. I told her to go upstairs and change down to the skin, and all she would do was laugh and say it didn't matter. It'll matter all right when she gets pneumonia. Didn't you notice the rain?"

"Not really," said Charlotte.

Lily produced a dry towel, removed Charlotte's spectacles, carefully dried the lenses, and then gently put them on again, setting them straight across the bridge of Charlotte's small nose. Using the same towel, she began to dry the child's hair, rubbing as though she were drying a wet puppy, scolding on. I left them to it and went to take off the mackintosh and the sou'wester and drape them over the radiator in the hall to dry.

The door to Phoebe's sitting room stood open. On the far side the fire blazed, the flames reflected in the brass fender and on all the little polished knickknacks that stood about—a copper jug, a silver photograph frame, a luster bowl. In front of the fire, with an elbow on the mantelpiece and a foot on the fender, stood Daniel. The profile of his downcast face was reflected in the mirror that hung above the mantelpiece, and in his hand he held a sheet of paper, which he appeared to be studying.

I came through the door, and he looked up.

"I've got Charlotte. She's with Lily, getting dried. She was looking for blackberries." I went to stand beside him, spreading my cold hands to the warmth of the fire. "What are you looking at?"

"This little picture she's done. She's very good."

He handed it to me and moved away from the fireplace to sink, recumbent, in the roomy depths of Chips's old armchair. He looked tired, his chin sunk on his chest, his long legs stretched out in front of him. I looked at Charlotte's drawing and saw at once what he meant. It was a child's effort, but imaginative and cleanly drawn. She had used felt pens, and the bright primary colours reminded me of Phoebe's own brilliant little oils. I saw the red boat bowling across a cobalt sea, the sail curved and set full in the wind. There was a small figure at the helm wearing a cap with a sea-going peak, and on the foredeck a large, whiskery cat.

I smiled. "I like the cat."

"I like the whole thing."

"It's a very cheerful picture. And that's odd, because I don't think she's a particularly cheerful child."

"I know," said Daniel. "It's reassuring."

I put the drawing on the mantelpiece, propped against Phoebe's clock. "Tomorrow I said I'd take her somewhere. She isn't having much of a time with her grandmother. I thought we could go somewhere in the car."

"That would be kind."

"She seemed to think it would be more fun if you came, too."

"Did she," said Daniel. He did not seem over-excited at the prospect. I wondered if he was already tiring of feminine company, or perhaps the idea of a day spent with Charlotte and myself had no allure for him. I wished now that I had said nothing about it. "You've probably got better things to do."

He said, "Yes," and then, "We'll see."

We'll see. He sounded like the adults who used to infuriate me as a child by using those very words when they were unable, or possibly unwilling, to commit themselves.

Chips had made the carousel for me. It was mine. He had said when he gave it to me that if I wanted, I could take it back to London, but I chose not to. The carousel was part of Holly Cottage, and I was such a traditionalist that I chose to leave it here.

It lived where it always had, in the bottom half of the huge French bombe cabinet that stood at one end of Phoebe's sitting room. That evening, after tea had been cleared away and washed up, Charlotte went to take it out. She carried it carefully and set it on the table in front of the fire.

Chips had made it from an old-fashioned gramophone. He had removed the lid and the needle arm and cut a circle of plywood the same size as a regular record, with a hole in the middle to fit over the gramophone's central spindle. This disc was painted a bright scarlet, and the animals were fixed around its perimeter. These, too, had been cut from plywood with Chips's little jigsaw. There was a tiger, an elephant, a zebra, a pony, a lion, and a dog, each coloured with its own stripes or spots and each sporting a brightly painted saddle with tiny bridles and reins made of golden cord.

Various games could be played with it. Sometimes, along with building blocks, farmyard people, and a few wooden animals left over from a defunct Noah's Ark, it became part of a fairground or a circus. But mostly I played with it just as it was, winding the handle to power the mechanism and switching the lever that made the turntable revolve. There was, as well, another lever to regulate the speed. You could start it up very slowly (to give people time to get on, Chips used to say) and then speed it up until the animals whirled so fast you could scarcely see them.

Charlotte did this now. It was like watching a spinning top. Finally the mechanism ran down, and the carousel came slowly to a halt.

She crouched down on her heels and moved the turntable with her hand, gazing at the face of each animal in turn.

"I simply don't know *which* is my favorite."

"The tiger was always mine," I told her. "He has such a fierce face."

"I know. He's a bit like the tigers in *Little Black Sambo*, isn't he. And you know, when the animals go round really fast they look a bit like the *Little Black Sambo* tigers going round the tree and turning into butter."

"Perhaps," said Phoebe, "Lily made our pancakes out of tiger butter, just the way Little Black Sambo's mother did."

"Why did you have to make old-fashioned gramophones go fast and slow? I mean, there's everything on my father's stereo at home, in Sunningdale, but I don't think there's a switch to make it go fast or slow."

"It was great fun," Phoebe told her. "You could put an ordinary record on very slowly and it sounded like an enormous Russian singing basso profundo. And then you'd make it go quickly and

it was all squeaky and high. Like a mouse singing."

"But *why*? Why did that happen?"

Phoebe said, "I haven't the faintest idea,"
which was always her very sensible reply to a question to which she had no answer.

Charlotte turned to me. "Do you know?"

"No, I don't."

"Do you?" She turned to Daniel.

He had been silent all this time. He had, for
that matter, been silent through most of tea. Now
he was back in Chips's armchair, apparently
watching the carousel with the rest of us and yet
in some way remote and withdrawn. Now we all
looked at him expectantly, but he had not even
realised that Charlotte had spoken to him, and
she had to say it again. "Do you, Daniel?"

"Do I what?"

"Do you know why the music goes squeaky
when it's fast and basso profundo when it's slow?"

He considered this question with some care and
then suggested that perhaps it had something to
do with centrifugal force.

Charlotte screwed up her nose. "What's *that*?"

"It's what makes your spin dryer work."

"I haven't got a spin dryer."

"Well, when you're a big girl, perhaps you'll

have one, and you'll look at it working, and then you'll know what centrifugal force is."

Charlotte began to wind the gramophone handle again. Above us, on the mantelpiece, Phoebe's clock struck five.

Phoebe said gently, "Charlotte, perhaps it's time you went home."

"Oh, do I *have* to?"

"No, you don't have to, but I said you'd be back about five."

Charlotte looked up, her expression all set to whine. "I don't want to go. And I can't walk back, because it's raining."

"Prue will take you in my car."

"Aw . . ."

Terrified of tears, I said quickly, "And don't forget, we've got a date for tomorrow. We're going out together in the car. Do you want me to come and fetch you?"

"No. I hate being fetched because I hate waiting. I'm always afraid people won't come. I'll come here. I'll walk down like I did this morning. What time shall I be here?"

"Oh, about half past ten?"

"All right."

Daniel had heaved himself to his feet. "Where are you off to?" Phoebe asked him.

"I must go, too," he told her.

"But I thought you were going to stay for dinner with Prue and me. Lily's made a chicken casserole . . ."

"No, really . . . I should get back. I've got a phone call to make. I promised Peter Chastal I'd get in touch with Lewis Falcon, and I've done nothing about it . . ."

"Oh, all right," said Phoebe, who always instantly accepted other people's decisions and never tried to argue. "Then you'd better go with Prue, and she'll drive you back to Porthkerris after she's dropped Charlotte."

He looked at me. "Do you mind?"

"Of course not."

But I did mind, because I wanted him to want to have dinner with Phoebe and me.

"Good-bye, Phoebe." He went to give her a kiss, and she gave him an affectionate little pat on the arm; letting him go, asking no questions.

That's the way I've got to be, I told myself, as I went to fetch my coat. *If I don't want to lose his friendship that's the way I've got to be.*

In the car, he sat in front, while Charlotte perched on the backseat, leaning forward so that the pale blur of her face hung between us.

"Where shall we go tomorrow?" she wanted to know.

"I don't know. I hadn't thought. Where's a good place?"

"We could go up to Skadden Hill. We'd maybe find blackberries. And there's lots of rocks on the top of the hill and one of them has got a giant's footprint on it. Really. A real, huge footprint."

Daniel said, "You could go to Penjizal."

"What happens at Penjizal?" I asked.

"There's a cliff walk, and at low tide a great deep rock pool, and the seals come into it and swim there."

Charlotte instantly forgot about Skadden Hill. Giant's footsteps were tame compared to seals.

"Oh, let's go there. I've never seen seals, at least not close to."

I said, "I don't even know where Penjizal is."

"Will you show us, Daniel?" Charlotte banged on his shoulder with her fist to get his whole attention. "Will you come with us? Oh, do come with us."

Daniel did not at once respond to this impassioned appeal. I knew that he was waiting for me to intervene, perhaps make some excuse for him, but I stayed selfishly silent. Through the windscreen wipers' fan of clear glass I saw the road ahead, awash with muddy water; the oak trees, black against the sky, lashed with rain.

"Please," Charlotte persisted.

He said, "I might."

But she stuck to her guns. "Does that mean yes or no?"

"Well, all right . . ." He turned his head to grin at her. "Yes."

"Oh, *good.*" She actually clapped her hands. "What shall I bring, Prue? Shall I bring my gum boots?"

"Perhaps you'd better. And a proper raincoat in case it's wet."

"But we'll have a picnic, won't we, even if it's raining?"

"Yes, we'll have a picnic. We'll find somewhere to eat it. What do you like? Ham sandwiches?"

"Yes. And Coke."

"I don't think we've got any Coke."

"I think Granny's got some. And if she hasn't I'll go and buy some. They sell it in the village shop."

We had reached the gates of White Lodge. I drove through them and up the short drive, and the house, as before, waited for us, curtained in the rain, its face closed and blank, giving nothing away. We drew up at the foot of the steps, and

Daniel got out in order to let Charlotte emerge from the backseat. He stood looking down at her. She was holding the picture she had drawn. Phoebe had taken it down from the mantelpiece and given it to Charlotte as we were on the point of leaving.

"Don't forget this," she had said, and added hopefully, "Perhaps you'd like to give it to your grandmother."

But now Charlotte held it out to Daniel. "Would you like to keep it?" she asked him shyly.

"I'd like to very much. But isn't it for your grandmother?"

"Not really. She won't want it."

"In that case, I'll take it." He did so. "Thank you. I shall treasure it."

"I'll see you tomorrow then. Good-bye. Good-bye, Prue, and thank you for bringing me home."

We watched her climb the steps to the front door. As Daniel got back into the car beside me, the door opened. A wedge of yellow light shone out into the murk, and we saw Mrs. Tolliver standing there. She waved—perhaps to say thank you, perhaps to say good-bye—and then drew Charlotte indoors.

Chapter 5

WE SET OFF FOR PORTHKERRIS. It was only a short journey, but it was made that evening, by Daniel and me, in total silence. Sometimes silences between two people are comfortable things; sometimes they speak more loudly than words. On other occasions they become strained and tense, and this was one of them. I wanted to break the constraint, to start some trivial conversation, but in the face of such noncooperation I could think of no words for the tall, quiet stranger who sat beside me. His hand, still holding Charlotte's present, lay against his knee. His head was turned away from me. He stared out at the drenched, grey-green fields, the stony walls, the rain. There seemed to be nothing to say.

We reached the gates of the hotel at last, turned up the driveway, parked with all the expensive cars. On that gloomy evening even the opulent Castle Hotel had an abandoned appearance, like a sinking liner, with its few lighted windows reflected in a sea of puddles.

I turned off the engine and waited for Daniel to get out of the car. Now there was only the sound of the rain drumming on the roof and the sough of wind blown up from the sea far below us. Listening, I heard the distant breakers crashing on the shore. Daniel turned his head and looked at me. "Will you come in?"

I couldn't think why he had even bothered to ask me. "No. You have to get in touch with Lewis Falcon. And I should get back . . ."

He said urgently, "Please. I want to talk to you."

"What about?"

"We can have a drink."

"Daniel . . ."

"Please, Prue."

I switched off the headlights and we got out of the car. Once more the revolving doors injected us into that warm, scented, carpeted, overheated interior. Today, perhaps because of the inclement weather, there were more people about. They sat grouped around tea tables, read their newspapers, chatted over knitting. The air was thick with late-afternoon boredom. Daniel headed for the bar, but it was too early and it had not opened yet.

He stopped before the shuttered door and said, "Bloody hell," so loudly that one or two pairs of eyes were raised to observe us. I felt embarrassed. I knew how we looked, untidy and incongruous; Daniel in his worn jeans and the sweater of dark rough wool; myself in an old navy blue duffle coat that had seen better days, and with my hair wind-blown and uncombed.

I wanted to go away. "I don't want a drink, anyway."

"I do. Come on, we'll go up to my room."

And without waiting for my response to this suggestion, he set off up the wide staircase, his long legs taking the steps three at a time. Because there didn't seem to be anything else to do, I followed him, aware of the interest that our behaviour was arousing. I knew that we would be suspected of the very worst, but so concerned was I by Daniel's behaviour, so apprehensive for myself, that I didn't care anyway.

His room was on the first floor, at the end of a

long, wide passage. He took the key from his
pocket and went in, turning on the lights, and I
followed him and saw that he had been given one
of the best rooms in the hotel, facing out over the
small nine-hole golf course. The greens and fair-
ways of this golf course sloped to a little wood,
and so high on the hill were we that the sea's
horizon lay above the topmost branches of these
trees. This evening the horizon was not visible,
but the window of Daniel's room stood open, and
the wind poured in upon us and sent the long
curtains flapping like badly set sails.

He shut the door and went to close the window. The curtains ceased their frantic dance. I
looked at the large, comfortably furnished room,
with its unexpected features that made it feel
more like a bedroom in some well-loved country
house than an impersonal hotel. There was a fireplace, and over this a pretty mirror, framed in
rose-colour glass. Chintz-covered armchairs were
drawn up before the fireplace, and the same
chintz skirted the dressing table. A television set
stood on a low table, and beside this was a small
refrigerator. There were even flowers on the mantelpiece and a round basket of fresh fruit by the
wide double bed.

When he had shut the window, Daniel went to

switch on the electric fire. Sham logs instantly flickered. He was still holding Charlotte's picture. Now he placed it carefully in the middle of the mantelpiece. In the mirror I could see his quiet reflected face.

I watched him and waited.

He said, "She's my child."

Beyond his reflection, I could see my own, my face a pale blur, my hands deep in the pockets of my coat; the whole image distorted by some flaw in the glass so that I appeared ghostly, like a person drowned.

It was suddenly very hard to speak. I said, "Charlotte," and the word came out as a whisper.

"Yes, Charlotte." He turned from the fireplace, and across the room our eyes met. "She's my child."

"But why are you saying this?"

He said again, "She's my child."

"Oh, Daniel."

"You see, all those years ago, I had a love affair with her mother. I wasn't in love with Annabelle, she was married to another man, she already had a child. Everything was against us. But still, contrary to any sort of reason, it happened. And Charlotte is the outcome of a long, hot summer of what must have been total madness."

I said, "I know about it. I mean, I know about you and Annabelle Tolliver."

"Phoebe told you."

"Yes."

"I thought she might tell you. In fact, I was pretty sure that she would."

We stared at each other. My mind, like a panicky rabbit, scuttled to and fro, getting nowhere. I tried to remember the words that Phoebe had used. *I think it was Annabelle who fancied Daniel. Daniel was a very quiet person. It was a total non-event anyway.*

I said. "But I thought . . . I mean . . . I didn't realise . . ."

He rescued me from my delicate floundering. "You thought we'd just had a little walk out. I always hoped that that was what Phoebe and Chips thought too. But you see, it wasn't nearly as innocent as that."

"You're . . . you're sure she's your child?"

"I knew the moment I saw her this afternoon, sitting there on her camp stool, at the end of the sea wall. In the cold and the rain, trying to finish her picture. Prue, you've gone as white as a sheet. I think we'd better both have a drink."

I watched him go to open the refrigerator. He took out glasses and ice and soda water and a bottle of whisky and set these on the top of the cabinet.

"Daniel, I don't drink whisky."

"I haven't anything else." He unscrewed the top of the bottle.

I said, "She doesn't even look like you."

"She doesn't look like Annabelle, either. But I have a photograph of my mother when she was just about that age. Nine or ten. Charlotte is my mother all over again."

"Did you know that Annabelle was having your baby?"

"She said she was."

"Wasn't that enough?"

"As things turned out, no."

"I don't understand."

He shut the refrigerator door and stood leaning against it, a tumbler in either hand. "Prue, take off your coat. It makes you look impermanent. Besides, it's probably damp. You mustn't catch a cold."

I thought this the most irrelevant observation, but I did as he said, unbuttoning the coat and taking it off and laying it over the back of a chair. He held out my drink and I went to take it from him. The glass was icily cold.

I said again, "I don't understand, Daniel."

"You can't understand unless you understand about Annabelle." He frowned. "Did you never meet her? When you were staying with Phoebe?"

"No, our paths never crossed. I suppose because she used to come down in the summer, and I was usually in Northumberland then, with my father."

"That would explain it."

"Were you in love with her?" I sounded cool, as if it were of no importance.

"No, I wasn't in love with her. Come to think of it, I didn't even like her very much. But there was something . . . amazing about Annabelle that rendered every other emotion meaningless. I was twenty and she was twenty-eight. Married and a mother. None of that mattered, either."

"But didn't people . . . talk? Surely Phoebe and Chips . . ."

"They knew, of course, but they imagined it was just a jolly flirtation. And Annabelle was clever. She played the field. There were always plenty of other men."

"She must have been very beautiful." It was hard to keep the wistful note from my voice, but I had never been described as "amazing" and knew that I never would be.

"No, she wasn't beautiful. But she was very tall

and slender and she had a face like a Siamese cat, with a neat little nose and a long upper lip and a smile that was full of secrets. 'Enigmatic,' perhaps, the word is. Her eyes were astonishing. Enormous, slanted, a very dark grey.''

"How did you meet her?"

"Phoebe and Chips carted me off to this party. I didn't want to go, but they said I had to, I'd been invited, and I'd get boring if I did nothing but work. And Annabelle was there. I saw her the moment I walked into the room. She was over on the far side, surrounded by other women's husbands. I saw that face and my fingers itched to draw her. I suppose I was staring, because she suddenly looked up, straight at me, as though she'd known all along that I was there. And I forgot about drawing her." He gave a rueful grin and shook his head. "It was like playing a game of rugger and then getting a great kick in the guts.''

"That's never happened to me."

I hoped my timid attempt at levity would make him smile, but he didn't seem to hear it, for now he was pacing up and down the room with his glass in his hand as though it were physically impossible for him to talk and stand still at the same time.

"The next time we met, it was on the beach. I'd

got a surfboard, a Malibu, from Australia. A friend had brought it for me from Sydney. There was a north wind that day, and the rollers were pouring in from miles out. I surfed until the tide changed, and when I came in, blue with cold because I couldn't afford a wet suit, I saw Annabelle sitting up on the dunes, watching me. I had no idea how long she'd been there. She wore a red skirt and her hair was loose and black and blowing in the wind. There wasn't anyone else on the beach that grey day, and I knew that she was waiting for me. So I climbed up to where she sat, and we talked and smoked her cigarettes, and the rushes all around us were flattened by the gale. I remember thinking that they looked like stroked fur. And later we walked home, and the golf links smelled of wild thyme. And a couple of men, golfers, passed us, and I saw them looking at Annabelle and then at me, and there was envy in their faces. It made me feel good. And that's the way it always was; going into a pub with her, or sitting beside her in the car, with the roof down and the sun on our faces. We'd stop at traffic lights, and people on the pavements would turn their heads, and stare, and smile."

"They were probably thinking what a good-looking couple you made."

"More likely asking themselves what a sensational creature like Annabelle was doing with a callow, gangling boy."

"How long did this go on for?"

"Two months. Three months. It was a very hot summer. She said it was too hot to take her little boy back to London. So she stayed at Penmarron. She was always there."

"Did she talk about her husband?"

"Leslie Collis? Not much. Rumour had it that she'd married him for his money, and she certainly didn't talk of him with much obvious affection. That didn't bother me. I didn't want to know about him. I didn't want to think about him. I didn't want to feel guilty. If you're really determined, it's quite possible to stuff an uneasy conscience out of sight. I'd never realised that I had that ability. It made things much easier."

"Perhaps, at twenty, that's the way you're meant to live life."

He smiled. "You sound old and wise. Like Phoebe."

"I wish I were."

He was still pacing, a caged tiger, up and down the charming, pretty room. He said, "It was about this time of the year, the middle of September. Only it wasn't raining like it is now. They went on and on, the sunshine and the warmth. So that I was taken unawares when Annabelle suddenly announced that she was going back to London. We were on the beach again. We'd been swimming. It was a flood tide, one late afternoon. The tide had come in over the warm sand, and the sea was the colour of jade and very warm. We were sitting having a cigarette, and she told me about going back to London, and I waited for utter desolation, and then realised that I wasn't desolate. In a funny way, I was relieved. I wanted it to stop now, while we were still having fun. I didn't want it to get stale. Besides, I knew that I had to get back to work. Painting has always been the most important thing in my life, and it had started tugging at me. I wanted to turn my back on everything else and concentrate on my painting, drown myself in it. My year with Chips was just about over. I wanted to travel, to learn. I planned to go to America.

"I started to say something trivial, but Annabelle interrupted me. It was then that she told me she was having a baby. She said, 'It's your child, Daniel.'

"You know, when I was young, growing up, I used to scare the pants off myself by imagining just such a situation. A girl, pregnant by me. A girl I didn't want to marry. Paternity suits, furious fathers, shotgun weddings. Nightmarish. And now it had happened, only it wasn't happening that way. She went on talking, and it gradually sank into my paralysed brain that she wanted nothing of me. She didn't want me to act as correspondent for a divorce; didn't want me to elope; didn't want me to marry her. She didn't want money.

"I felt there had to be a catch in it somewhere. Finally, when she stopped talking, I said, 'What about your husband?' and Annabelle laughed and said that he wouldn't ask any questions. I told her I couldn't believe this; no man would accept another man's child. But Annabelle said that Leslie Collis would, to save his own face and his pride; he hated more than anything else in the world to be made to look foolish. He minded what his colleagues thought of him, what people said about him. He'd built up for himself this hard-headed image, and he would let nothing destroy it. And then she looked at the expression on my face and she laughed again, and she said, 'Don't worry, Daniel, he won't come gunning for you.'

"I said, 'But it's my baby,' and she threw her cigarette away and pushed her hair out of her face and said, 'Oh, don't bother about the baby. It'll have a good home,' and she made it sound as though she were talking about a dog."

He was still now, the restless pacing stopped. He stood in the middle of the room, looking down into his glass. There was still some whisky left in the bottom, and with a quick movement of hand and head, he tipped the last of it down his throat. I hoped that he would not pour himself another. He seemed to me, in this frame of mind, a man happy to drink himself into oblivion. But he went and put the empty glass back on top of the refrigerator and then, noticing that it was now dark, moved to the window and drew the heavy curtains, shutting away the dismal night outside.

He turned to face me. "You're not saying anything."

"I can't think of anything intelligent to say."

"You're shocked."

"That's a ludicrous word to use. I'm in no position to be shocked. I'm in no position to take up any sort of attitude. But for your sake, I'm sorry it happened."

"I haven't told you everything yet. Do you want to hear the rest?"

"If you want me to hear."

"I think I do. I . . . I haven't talked like this

for years. I'm not sure if I could stop now, even if I wanted to."

"Have you never told anyone before?"

"Yes. I told Chips. At first I thought I wouldn't. I couldn't. For one thing, I was too ashamed. Leslie Collis wasn't the only man who hated to look foolish. But I was never much good at hiding my feelings, and after a couple of days of idiocy, shambling around Chips's studio and dropping things, he lost patience with me and came out with it, and said what the hell was the matter with me, anyway. So I told him then. I told him everything, and he never interrupted; never said a word. Just sat there in his saggy old chair, smoking his pipe and listening. And when I'd finished, got it off my chest, the relief was so great that I couldn't think why I hadn't told him straight away."

"What did he say?"

"He didn't say anything for a bit. Just went on smoking and gazing into space. Mulling things over. I didn't know what he was thinking. I half-expected to be told to go and pack my bags and never darken the doors of Holly Cottage again.

"But finally he knocked the ash out of his pipe and put it in his pocket and said, 'Young man, you are being taken for a ride.' And then he told me about Annabelle. He said that she had always been amoral, openly promiscuous. That summer was no exception. As for the baby, there was another man, a farmer from over Falmouth way, married and with a family of his own. In Chips's opinion, there was every likelihood that he was the father of Annabelle's baby. And Annabelle must know this.

"When he came out with this, I was in more of a quandary than ever. Half of me was relieved. But, as well, I felt cheated. My pride was badly bruised. I knew I was deceiving Leslie Collis, but it gave my newly found manhood a kick in the teeth to be told that Annabelle had been two-timing me. That sounds despicable, doesn't it?"

"No. It's understandable. But if it was true, why did she say the baby was *yours?*"

"I asked Chips that very question. And he told me that that had always been Annabelle's way. It was no fun creating havoc if she couldn't leave behind her a trail of guilt and remorse. Unbelievable, isn't it?"

"It sounds unbelievable to me. But if Chips said that, then it has to be true."

"I knew that, too. He went and saw Annabelle that very evening. Had it out with her. He walked up to White Lodge and got Annabelle on his own.

At first she tried to bluff it out, insisting that it could be nobody's child but mine. But then he faced her with what he had told me. About the other man. And when he came out with his name, Annabelle broke down and admitted that he was right. It wasn't necessarily my child. She just liked to think that it might be. I never saw her again. She went back to London a couple of days later, taking the little boy and his nanny with her. And Chips and I agreed that it was time that I went, too. I'd been marking time for far too long."

"Does Phoebe know about all this?"

"No. I didn't want her to know, and Chips agreed that it would be better if she didn't. Hopefully, there would be no repercussions, and there was no point in upsetting her or creating any sort of trouble with Mrs. Tolliver. Penmarron is a small village. They had to go on living there, both of them part of a fairly tight community."

"What a wise man Chips was."

"Wise. Understanding. I can't begin to describe to you his kindness to me at that time. Like the very best sort of father. He fixed everything for me, even lent me some money to see me through till I found my feet. He gave me letters of introduction to friends of his in New York, but most important, he sent me off with a letter of introduction to Peter Chastal in London. In those days the gallery had been going only for a couple of years, but he'd already earned something of a name for himself in the art world. I took a great folio of my work for him to look at, and by the time I left for America, he'd agreed to exhibit for me and act as my agent. And that's what he's done ever since."

I thought of the ecstatic review I had read on the train. "He's done well for you."

"Yes. I've been fortunate."

"Chips used to say it was no good having a talent if you didn't work at it."

"Chips used to say a lot of sound things."

"Was it working that kept you away for eleven years?"

"I like to think so. I don't like to think I was trying to escape from what had happened. But perhaps I was. Running. Further and further away. New York first, and then Arizona, and then San Francisco. It was while I was there that I first became interested in Japanese art. There's a big Japanese community in San Francisco, and I found myself involved with a group of young painters. The longer I worked with them, the more I realised how little I knew. The traditions and disciplines of Japanese painting go back for centuries. It fascinated me. So I went to Japan, and there I became a student again, sitting at the feet of a very old and famous man. Time ceased to have any meaning. I was there for four years. Sometimes it seemed like a few days. At others, eternity.

"This exhibition at Peter Chastal's is a direct result of those years. I told you I didn't want to come back for it. Opening days do genuinely terrify me. But as well, I was afraid of coming back to England. On the other side of the world it was possible not to think about Annabelle and the child that might be mine. But coming back . . . I had nightmares about being in London and seeing Annabelle and my child walking up the pavement towards me."

"Wasn't coming to Cornwall something of a risk?"

"It all seemed predestined. Meeting a stranger in a pub, being offered a lift. I very nearly didn't come, but I wanted so much to see Phoebe again."

I thought back to yesterday. I remembered how quietly he had sat at the bar downstairs while I chattered on about Mrs. Tolliver and Charlotte. "Daniel, when I told you Charlotte was here, at Penmarron, staying with her grandmother, you must have realised that she was the baby."

"Yes, I realised. And I knew, too, for sure, inevitably, that I was going to meet her. It was all part of some extraordinary pattern, out of my control. When we got to Phoebe's this afternoon and got out of the car and went into the house, I knew that Charlotte was around, somewhere. I knew even before Lily told us. And as I walked out of the house and down the hill and along the seawall to fetch them back for tea, I kept telling myself that after all these years of uncertainty, I was finally going to know.

"They didn't notice me coming. They were both far too engrossed in their work. And then Phoebe caught sight of me and said my name. And Charlotte looked up, too. And there was that little face. And I knew then that, without knowing it, Annabelle had told me the truth."

So that was it. I seemed to have been standing forever, listening to Daniel's voice. My back ached, and I felt drained and exhausted. I had no idea what hour it was. From downstairs, from the busy heart of the hotel, came sounds and smells. Voices, the distant clash of dishes, the thin strains of an orchestra playing something undemanding out of *The Sound Of Music*. Sometime I had to return to Holly Cottage, to Phoebe and the chicken casserole. But not yet.

I said, "If I don't sit down I shall die." And I went over to the fireplace and collapsed in one of the chintz-covered armchairs. All the time we had talked the little fake flames had licked cheerfully around the pretend logs. Now I sat back, with my chin buried in the collar of my sweater, and watched them flickering busily, getting nowhere.

I heard Daniel pour himself another drink. He brought it over and sat facing me in the other chair. I looked up, and our eyes met. We were both very solemn.

I smiled. "So now you've told me. And I don't know why you told me."

"I had to tell someone. And for some reason, you seem to be part of it all."

"No. I'm not part of it." It was about the only thing of which I was certain. Otherwise the situation in which Daniel now found himself seemed to have no solution. I thought about it for a bit and then went on. ". . . and I don't think that you're part of it, either. It's over, Daniel. Finished. Forgotten. Water under the bridge. You thought that Charlotte might be your child; now you know that she is. That's all that's changed. Charlotte is still Charlotte Collis, Leslie Collis's daughter, Mrs. Tolliver's granddaughter, and Phoebe's friend. Accept that and forget about everything else. Because there really is no alternative. The fact that you've discovered the truth is irrelevant. It alters nothing. Charlotte was never your responsibility and she isn't now. You have to think of her as a little girl you met on the seawall who happens to share your talent for drawing and whose face reminds you of your mother's."

He did not answer me at once. And then he said, "If that were all I had to come to terms with, it wouldn't be so bad."

"What do you mean, exactly?"

"I mean exactly what you observed in the train, and what Lily Tonkins, who is nobody's fool, instantly put her finger on. Charlotte not only has to wear spectacles, but she bites her fingernails, she is lonely, she is unhappy and apparently neglected."

I looked away from him, turning to the fire for diversion. If it had been a proper one, I could have filled in the difficult moment by some small business with a poker or a fresh log. As it was, I found myself at a loss. I knew, and Phoebe knew and Lily Tonkins knew, that everything Daniel had just said was in all probability true. But to agree with him now could do no good for Charlotte and would only make the situation even more difficult for Daniel to accept.

I sighed, searching for words. "You mustn't take everything that Lily says quite literally. She's always been inclined to overdramatize things. And you know, little girls of Charlotte's age aren't always very easy to understand. They become secretive and withdrawn. As well, I think she's rather a shy child . . ."

I looked up and met his gaze again. I smiled, making my face cheerful and matter-of-fact. ". . . And let's face it, Mrs. Tolliver would never win a competition for the world's coziest granny. That's why Charlotte's so fond of Phoebe. And anyway, I don't suppose she's having a bad time staying at White Lodge. I know there are no other children to play with, but that's because all the other children in the village are back at school. And despite what Lily said, I'm sure Betty Curnow spends a bit of time with her and is kind. You mustn't let things exaggerate themselves in your mind. Besides, tomorrow we're taking her out for a picnic. You haven't forgotten that, have you? You said you'd take us to Penjizal and show us the seals . . . you can't back out now."

"No. I won't back out."

"I understand why you were reluctant to come with us. It won't be very easy for you."

He shook his head. "I don't see that a single

day is going to make much difference, one way or another, taken in the context of two separate lifetimes."

I tried to work this out. "I don't know what that means, but I'm sure you're right."

He laughed. Downstairs the orchestra had switched from *The Sound Of Music* to *The Pirates of Penzance*. I could smell delicious food.

I said, "Come back with me. To Holly Cottage. Phoebe would love it so much. We'll eat Lily's casserole, the way we planned. She's cooked enough to feed an army."

But he said that he would not come.

I looked at the empty whisky glass on the floor between his feet.

"You promise me you won't sit here all evening and drink yourself into a coma?"

He shook his head. "How little you know me. How little we know each other. I don't drink that way. I never have."

"But you'll get something to eat? You'll have dinner?"

"Yes. Later. I'll go downstairs."

"Well, if you won't come, then I must go on my own. Phoebe will think I've forgotten about her or crashed the car or something ghastly."

I got out of my chair and so did Daniel. We

stood, like people at a formal party when it is time to leave.

"Good night, Daniel."

He put his hands on my shoulders and stooped to kiss my cheek. When he had done this, I stood for a long moment, looking up into his face. I put my arms around his neck and drew his head down to mine and kissed his mouth. I felt his arms come around me, felt myself held so close that I could feel the beating of his heart through the thick, rough wool of his sweater.

"Oh, Prue."

I laid my cheek against his shoulder. Felt his lips caress the top of my head. It was the most gentle of embraces, without passion, without apparent significance. So why did I suddenly feel this way, aching with a need I had never known before, my legs weak, my eyes burning with ridiculous, unshed tears? Could loving a person happen so suddenly? Like a rocket, fired into a dark sky, exploding into infinity and carrying with it a trail of shimmering, many coloured stars.

We stood silent, holding each other, like children clinging for comfort. It didn't seem to matter about not talking. Then Daniel said, "That house in Greece. I don't want you to think I didn't mean it when I asked you to come and visit me."

"Are you asking me to come with you now?"

"No."

I drew away from him and looked up into his face. He told me, "I can't go on running away from the inside of my own head. Maybe someday, sometime." He kissed me again, briskly this time, becoming practical, glancing at his wristwatch. "You must go. The casserole will be burned to nothing and Phoebe will think I've ravished you." He fetched my coat from the chair and held it out for me, and I put my arms into the sleeves, and he turned me around and did up all the buttons down the front.

"I'll come downstairs with you." He went to open the door, and we walked together, side by side, down the long corridor towards the head of the stairs. We passed rows of closed bedroom doors behind which people we had never known had loved and honeymooned and holidayed and laughed, and quarrelled and made up the quarrels with laughter.

The foyer, when we reached the foot of the stairs, now presented its most festive face. Guests emerged from the bar or made their way towards the restaurant or sat around those same little tables with cocktails before them and dishes of nuts. The hum of conversation, raised in order to be audible above the sound of the orchestra, was considerable. The men wore black ties and velvet dinner jackets, and the ladies were in evening skirts or sequinned caftans.

We walked through it all, causing a slight stir with our unexpected appearance, like ghosts at a feast. Conversations faltered as we walked by; eyebrows once more were raised. We reached the main door and were turned out into the darkness and the night. It had stopped raining at last, but there was still a wind keening through the high branches of trees.

Daniel looked up at the sky. "How will it be tomorrow?"

"Fine, perhaps. The wind may blow all the bad weather away."

We came to the car. He opened the door for me. "When shall I meet you?"

"About eleven. I'll come for you, if you want."

"No. I'll get a lift over to Penmarron or catch a bus or something. But I'll be there, so don't go without me."

"We have to have you there, to show us the way."

I got into the car, behind the wheel.

He said, "I'm sorry about this evening."

"I'm glad you told me."

"I'm glad, too. Thank you for listening."

"Good night, Daniel."

"Good night."

He slammed the door shut, and I started the engine and set off down the curving drive, following the beam of the headlights; away from him. I do not know how long he stood there after I had gone.

Chapter 6

WE TALKED THAT EVENING, Phoebe and I, far into the night. We indulged in memories, recalling the days when Chips was alive. We went even further back, to Northumberland, to Windyedge, where Phoebe had spent her childhood, running wild and riding her shaggy pony along the margins of those cold and northern beaches. We spoke of my father, and the contentment he had found with his new wife, and she remembered expeditions when they were all children together, to Dunstanbrugh and Bambrugh, and midwinter meets, with the pink coats of the huntsmen bright as berries in the frosty air and the foxhounds streaming across the snow-streaked fields.

We talked about Paris, where she had been a student, and the little house in the Dordogne she and Chips had bought one affluent year and to which she still returned for annual painting trips.

We talked about Marcus Bernstein, my job, my little flat in Islington.

"Next time I come to London, I shall come and stay with you," she promised.

"I haven't got a spare room."

"Then I shall sleep on the floor."

She told me about the new Society of Arts that had just been formed in Porthkerris and of which she was a founding member. She described for me the house of an old and famous potter, who had returned to Porthkerris to spend his final years in the warren of narrow streets where he had been born eighty years before, the son of a fisherman.

We talked about Lewis Falcon.

But we did not speak of Daniel. As though we had made some secret agreement, neither Phoebe nor I mentioned his name.

Past midnight she went at last to bed. I followed her up the stairs to draw her curtains and turn down the quilt and help her off with her more awkward clothes. I took a hot-water bottle downstairs and filled it from the boiling kettle and finally left her, warm in her huge and downy bed, reading her book.

We said good night, but I did not go to bed. My mind was seething, as alert and restless as if I had pumped myself with some enormously stimulating drug. I could not face lying in the darkness, waiting for sleep that I knew would not come. So I returned to the kitchen and made a mug of coffee and took it back to the fireside. The flames had died to a bed of grey ash, so I threw on more logs and watched them kindle and flare, and then curled myself up into Chips's old armchair. Its battered depths were comforting, and I thought about him and longed for his presence. I did not want him dead; I wanted him alive, here, in this room with me. We had always been very close, and now I needed him. I needed his counsel.

Like the very best sort of father. I thought of Chips, his pipe in his mouth, listening as the young Daniel told him about Annabelle Tolliver and the baby. Annabelle, with her dark hair and her cat face and her grey eyes and her secret smile.

It's your child, Daniel.

There were other voices. Lily Tonkins. *Mrs. Tolliver can't be bothered to look after the child, then she should pay some other person to do the job.* Lily shrill with indignation, beating out her resentment on a bowl of batter.

And my mother, exasperated because I would not conform to the pattern that she had endeavoured all her life to cut for me.

Honestly, Prue, I don't know what you're looking for.

I had told her that I wasn't looking for anything. But there was a word—"serendipity." It was such an odd, strange-sounding word that I had once looked it up in a dictionary.

serendipity *n:* faculty of making happy discoveries by accident

I had discovered. Daniel. Watched him walking from the little railway station, along the old seawall, towards me, into my life. This evening, "How little we know each other," he had said, and up to a point, that was true. A day. Two days. Too short, one would have said, to achieve anything but the most superficial relationship.

But this was different. For me time and events had become miraculously encapsulated, so that I felt as though I had lived an entire lifetime with him in the course of the past twenty-four hours. It was hard to realise that I had not known him forever, that our two separate existences were not already spun together, like strands in a single skein of wool.

I wanted it to go on being this way. I was prepared to let him go his way, as Phoebe had let him go. I was wise enough for that. But I did not want to lose him. And I knew that the odds were against me. Partly because Daniel was the man that he was—an artist, restless, seeking, he would always need to be free. But infinitely more formidable was the memory of Annabelle, the existence of Charlotte.

Charlotte. Who knew what traumas Charlotte had suffered, foisted upon a man who was not her father and who must surely know that he was not her father. I had taken an instant dislike to him during those brief moments I had seen him on the train, watched his impatience with the little girl and recognised a total lack of affection as he thrust the ten-pound note into her hand, as though he were paying off some tiresome debt.

And Annabelle. So much unhappiness to answer for. *It was no fun creating havoc if she couldn't leave behind her a trail of guilt and remorse.* She had done that, all right, with her wayward passions, destructive as a hurricane. Now the hurricane seemed to have blown up again, and I was afraid

because I could see it tearing Daniel and me apart
forever.

*I can't go on running away from the inside of my
own head.*

I thought of the house in Greece, the sugar-
cube house above the sea, with the whitewashed
terrace and the bright geraniums. A scrap of po-
etry, half-learned, half-forgotten, flew like a ghost
through the back of my mind.

Oh, love, we two shall go no more to lands of
summer beyond the seas.

From the mantelpiece, Phoebe's clock chimed a
single, silvery note. One o'clock. I laid down the
empty coffee mug and with an effort pulled myself
from the deep comfort of Chips's armchair. Still
not sleepy, I went over to Phoebe's radio and fid-
dled with knobs, searching for some early-hour
music. I found a recorded programme of classic
pop, recognised a tune that dated back to the
years of my growing up.

God bless you,
You made me feel brand new
For God blessed me with you.

The toy carousel still stood on the table where Charlotte had played with it. It had never been put back in its cupboard, and now I went to do this, for fear that dust should seep into its ancient mechanism and cause it to grind to a final halt. I couldn't bear to think of it broken, forgotten, never played with again.

I simply don't know which is my favourite . . .

I wound the handle and gently released the lever. Slowly, sedately, the brightly painted animals revolved, their tinselly bridles sparkling in the light from the fire, like decorations on a Christmas tree.

Without you,
Life has no meaning or rhyme
Like notes to a song out of time.

There was always tomorrow. I could not be sure whether I dreaded the day we had planned or looked forward to it. There seemed to be too much at stake. I only knew that we would go, the three of us, to Penjizal and look for the seals. Beyond tomorrow I could not imagine, simply hope that some good would come of our being together. For Daniel's sake. For Charlotte. And, selfishly, for myself.

The mechanism ran down; the turntable slowly came to a halt. I stooped and lifted the carousel off the table and put it away in its cupboard; closed the doors, turned the key. I put the guard in front of the fire, switched off the radio, turned off the light. In the darkness, I went upstairs.

I awoke early, at seven, to the sound of a big old herring gull screaming at the new day from the roof of Chips's studio. My drawn curtains framed a sky of the palest blue veiled in a haze reminiscent of the hottest days of summer. There was no wind, no sound but the cry of the gull and the whisper of an incoming tide, trickling to fill the gullies and sand pools of the estuary. When I got up and went to the window, it was very cold, almost as though there had been a frost. I smelt the seaweed, tarry rope, and the clean saltiness of fresh seawater surging in from the ocean. It was a day made to order for a picnic.

I dressed and went downstairs and made coffee for myself and breakfast for Phoebe. When I took this up to her, I found her already awake and sitting up against the pillows, not reading but simply gazing with pleasure as the warmth of the sun on that perfect autumn morning burned away the last of the mist.

I put the breakfast tray on her knees.

"These are the sort of mornings," she said without preamble, "that I'm certain one remembers when one is very, very old. Good morning, my darling." We kissed. "What a day for a picnic."

"Come with us, Phoebe."

She was tempted. "It depends where you're going."

"Daniel's going to show us the way to Penjizal. He said something about a tidal rock pool where the seals come and swim."

"Oh, it's so beautiful! You'll be enchanted. But no, I think I'd better not come. The path down the cliffs is a little too precipitous for a person with only one arm. It would be too tiresome for you if I lost my balance and went flying over the cliff into the sea." She went into gales of her usual laughter at the very idea. "But the walk down from the farmhouse at the top is magical. There are wild fuchsias everywhere, and in summertime the valley is humming with dragonflies. What are you going to take with you to eat? Ham sandwiches? Have we got any ham? What a pity you can't make cold casserole sandwiches, there's so much left over from last night. I wonder if Daniel got in touch with Lewis Falcon. I've heard that he's got the most beautiful wild garden out there at Lanyon . . ."

She chattered on, her conversation, as always with Phoebe, darting from one intriguing subject to the next. It was tempting to forget about the day ahead; to lose all sense of time and simply to settle down to spending the rest of the morning sitting there on the end of Phoebe's downy bed. But, with the coffee pot empty and the sun's rays shining obliquely through the open window, I heard from downstairs the slamming of the kitchen door and knew that Lily Tonkins had arrived on her bicycle.

I looked at Phoebe's clock. "Heavens, it's past nine o'clock. I must get moving." I climbed reluctantly off the bed and started to gather up cups and plates, stacking them on Phoebe's tray.

"So must I."

"Oh, don't get up. Stay there for another hour or so. Lily likes it when you do that. She can get on with her polishing without having to shunt you around all the time."

"I'll see," said Phoebe, but as I went out the door, I saw her reach for her book. She was reading C. P. Snow, and I envied her her warm bed and that wonderful sonorous prose and guessed that it would be midday at least before she put in an appearance downstairs.

In the kitchen I found Lily tying on her apron.

"Hello, Prue, how are you this morning? Lovely, isn't it? Ernest said last night, this was what was going to happen. He said that wind was going to blow the dirty weather away. And coming down the road from the church, you'd think it was warm as June. Had a good mind not to come in to work today; just go down to the beach and put my feet in the tide."

From the hall, the telephone began to ring.

"Now," said Lily, as she invariably did when this happened, "who can that be?"

"I'll go," I said.

I went back to the hall and sat on the old carved chest where the telephone lived and picked up the receiver.

"Hello."

"Phoebe?" A woman's voice.

"No. This is Prue."

"Oh, Prue. This is Mrs. Tolliver. Is Phoebe there?"

"I'm afraid she's still in bed."

I expected her to apologise for the early call and to say that she would ring back later. But instead she persisted. "I must speak to her. Can she come to the telephone?" And there was an urgency to her voice, an unsteadiness, that filled me with nameless apprehension.

"Is anything wrong?"

"No. Yes. Prue—I have to talk to her."

"I'll get her." I laid down the receiver and went upstairs. As I put my head around Phoebe's door, she looked up placidly from her book.

"That's Mrs. Tolliver on the telephone. She wants to speak to you." I added, "She sounds very odd. Upset."

Phoebe frowned. "What's it about?" She laid down her book.

"I don't know." But my imagination had already scurried ahead. "Perhaps it's something to do with Charlotte."

Not hesitating any longer, Phoebe pushed back her covers and got out of bed. I helped her into her dressing gown, putting her good arm into the sleeve and wrapping the rest of its voluminous folds around her like a cape. I found her slippers. Her thick hair still lay in a plait over one shoulder, and her reading spectacles had slipped down her nose. She led the way down to the hall, sat where I had sat, picked up the receiver.

"Yes?"

The call was obviously important, and, possibly, private. Perhaps, realising this, I should have taken myself off out of earshot to the kitchen. But Phoebe sent me a glance that beseeched me to stay at hand, as though she expected to need my moral support, so halfway down the stairs, I sat, too, watching her through the bannister rails.

"Phoebe?" Mrs. Tolliver's voice was clearly audible from where I perched. "I'm sorry I had to get you out of bed, but I have to speak to you."

"Yes."

"I have to see you."

Phoebe looked a little nonplussed. "What, right away?"

"Yes. Now. Please. I . . . I think I need your advice."

"I hope Charlotte's all right?"

"Yes. Yes, she's all right. But please come. I . . . I really want to speak to you very urgently."

"I shall have to get dressed."

"Just come as soon as you can. I shall expect you." And before Phoebe could raise any objections, she had rung off.

Phoebe was left sitting there, holding the humming receiver. We looked at each other blankly, and I could tell by her face that she felt just as apprehensive as I did.

"Did you hear all that?"

"Yes."

Phoebe thoughtfully replaced the receiver, and the humming sound ceased.

"What on earth can be wrong? She sounds quite demented."

From the kitchen we could hear Lily wielding the floor polished and singing hymns. This was a sure sign that she was feeling on top of the world.

"Guard us, oh, thou Gre-hate Je-he-hovah . . ."

Phoebe stood up. "I'll have to go."

"I'll drive you in the car."

"You'd better help me get dressed first."

Back in her bedroom, she took from cupboards and drawers a selection of garments even more haphazard than usual. When she was ready, she sat at her dressing table, and I did her hair, replaiting it and winding it up into a knob at the back of her head, and holding it while she skewered it into place with her old-fashioned tortoiseshell pins.

I knelt to lace up her shoes. This done, "You go and get the car out," she told me. "I'll be down in a moment."

I found my coat and pulled it on and let myself out of the house. The pearly, brilliant morning shimmered all about me. I opened the garage and persuaded the old car to start. I had backed it out of the garage and was waiting by the front door when Phoebe appeared. She had put on one of her largest and most dashing hats, and, for warmth, had draped across her shoulders a brilliant poncho of wool, doubtless woven by some Middle Eastern peasant. Her spectacles were sliding down her nose; her hair, fresh from my inexpert hands, already looked as though it was about to collapse. None of this mattered. What did matter was that for once in her life she did not have a smile on her face, and this alone was enough to make me angry with Mrs. Tolliver.

She bundled herself into the seat beside me and we set off.

"What I can't understand," said Phoebe, giving her hat a tug to settle it even further down on her head, "is why me? I'm no particular friend of Mrs. Tolliver's. She's far more intimate with those nice ladies she plays bridge with. Perhaps it is something to do with Charlotte. She knows how fond I am of the child. That's it. It must be—" She stopped, abruptly. "Prue, why are we going so slowly? You're still in second gear." I changed up to third, and we continued our journey at a slightly increased speed. "We're meant to be in a hurry."

"I know," I said. "But I want to tell you something and I don't want to get to Mrs. Tolliver's before I've finished."

"What are you going to tell me?"

"It may have nothing to do with what she's going to talk about. But, on the other hand, I have an uncomfortable feeling that it has. I don't know whether I ought to say anything. But whether I ought to or not, I'm going to."

Phoebe sighed deeply. "It's about Charlotte, isn't it?"

"Yes. Daniel's her father."

Phoebe's worn hands stayed where they were, quietly clasped in her lap. "Did he tell you so?"

"Yes. He told me yesterday."

"You could have said something last night."

"He didn't ask me to."

We were moving so slowly that I had to change down again as the car ground on up the slight slope towards the church.

"So they did have an affair, he and Annabelle."

"Yes. You see, it wasn't just a little flingette after all. At the end of that summer, Annabelle told Daniel she was having his baby. And Daniel confided in Chips. And Chips pointed out that it wasn't necessarily Daniel's baby; it could easily be some other man's. And Chips confronted Annabelle with this, and she finally admitted to him that she couldn't be sure whose child it was."

"I always wondered why Daniel went off so precipitately to America. I mean, he'd been talking about it all summer, and I knew he planned to go. But all at once he was going. And then he'd gone."

"And didn't come back for eleven years."

"When did he realise she was his child?"

"As soon as he set eyes on her, sitting there on the seawall trying to finish her picture in the rain."

"*How* did he know?"

"Apparently she looks just the way his mother looked as a little girl."

"So there's no doubt."

"No. Not in Daniel's mind. No doubt."

Phoebe fell silent. Presently she sighed again, a long, troubled sigh. She said inadequately, "Oh, dear."

"I'm sorry, Phoebe. It's not a very nice thing to have to tell anyone."

"Perhaps in a strange way I already knew. I always had such a close relationship with Charlotte, just as I used to have with you. Just as I used to have with Daniel. And there were little things about her . . . mannerisms . . . that were strangely familiar. The way she holds a pencil, with her fingers all bunched up around it. Daniel holds a pencil that way."

"Chips never said anything to you?"

"Not a word."

"Perhaps I shouldn't have, either. But if you're going to be faced by some appalling revelation from Mrs. Tolliver, it's as well to have a few facts at your fingertips."

"I've got those all right. What a proper turn-up for the books." She added, without much hope, "Perhaps it's just going to be about the Women's Institute tea. And then your bombshell will have been all for nothing."

"It's not my bombshell. And if I hadn't told you, Daniel would have. And you know as well as I do that this isn't going to be about the Women's Institute tea."

There was no time for more. Even driving at my deliberate snail's pace, we had already covered the short distance between Holly Cottage and White Lodge. Here were the gates, the neatly kept drive, the gravel sweep in front of the formal house. But today the front door stood open, and as we drew up at the foot of the steps, Mrs. Tolliver came through the door and down the steps towards us. I wondered if she had been waiting for us just inside the hall, sitting on one of those ugly, uncomfortable chairs that are not meant to be used for sitting on but other purposes, like dumping overcoats and leaving parcels.

There was nothing outwardly dishevelled about her. I saw the usual well-cut skirt, the simple shirt, a cardigan of deep coral, the good pearls around her throat and set in the lobes of her ears, the well-coiffed grey hair.

But the inner turmoil was all too evident. She appeared distraught, her face blotched as though recently she had actually been crying.

Phoebe opened the door of the car.

"Phoebe, how good of you . . . how very good of you to come." She stooped to help Phoebe out and caught sight of me sitting behind the driving wheel. I smiled weakly.

"Prue had to come," said Phoebe briskly. "To drive me. You don't mind if she comes in, too, do you?"

"Oh . . ." Mrs. Tolliver obviously did mind, but it was a good indication of her immediate distress that this single word was as far as her objection went. "No. No, of course not."

I didn't want to go in in the very least. In the course of the last two days I'd had enough of the Tollivers, but Phoebe obviously wanted me with her, so trying to appear both disinterested and colourless, I too got out of the car and followed the two women up the stone steps and into the house.

The hall was flagged in stone, scattered with Persian rugs of great antiquity. A graceful staircase with a wrought-iron bannister curved to the upper floors. I closed the front door behind me, and Mrs. Tolliver led us across the hall and into her drawing room. She waited as we passed through the door and then closed it firmly, as though wary of possible eavesdroppers.

It was a large and formally furnished room, with long sash windows facing out onto the garden. The morning sun had not yet penetrated these windows, and the atmosphere was chilly. Mrs. Tolliver gave a shiver.

"It's cold. I hope you're not cold . . . so early . . ." Her instincts as a hostess rose to the surface. "Perhaps . . . light a fire . . . ?"

"I'm not in the least cold," said Phoebe. She chose a chair and sat firmly down in it, still bundled in her garish poncho and with her solid legs crossed at the ankle, like royalty. "Now, my dear. What is this about?"

Mrs. Tolliver crossed to the empty fireplace and

stood there, supporting herself with a hand laid along the edge of the mantelpiece.

"I . . . I really don't know where to begin . . ."

"Try the beginning."

"Well." She took a deep breath. "You know the reason Charlotte is with me?"

"Yes. The boiler at her school blew up."

"That, of course. But the real reason is that her mother—Annabelle—is in Majorca. That was why there was nobody to take care of her at home. Well . . . I had a telephone call last night, at about half past nine . . ."

She took her hand from the mantelpiece and felt up her cuff and produced a tiny, lace-edged handkerchief. As she went on talking, she played with this, looking to me as though she were trying to tear it to pieces.

"It was my son-in-law, Leslie Collis. Annabelle has left him. She's not coming back. She's with this man. He's a riding instructor. South African. She's going back to South Africa with him."

The enormity of her statement silenced the lot of us. I was thankful that I was expected to say nothing, but I looked at Phoebe. She sat unmoving, and I could not see the expression on her face, because it was obliterated by the brim of her hat.

At last, "I am so sorry," she said, and there was a whole world of sympathy in her voice.

"But you see, that isn't the end of it. I . . . I really don't know how I'm going to tell you."

"I imagine," said Phoebe, "that it's got something to do with Charlotte."

"He says that Charlotte is not his child. Apparently he always knew this, but he accepted her for Michael's sake, because he wanted to keep his home together. But he's never liked the child. I always knew that he never had any time for her, though of course I had no idea exactly why. It used to distress me when I stayed with them. He was so impatient with her, sometimes it seemed as though she could do nothing right."

"Did you say anything?"

"I didn't want to make trouble."

"She's always seemed to me to be rather a lonely little girl."

"Yes. Lonely. She never fit in. And she was never pretty and engaging, the way Annabelle used to be. I don't want you to think that Leslie was *unkind* to her. It was just that all his time and affection seemed to be centred on Michael . . . and there wasn't enough left over for Charlotte."

"What about her mother?"

Mrs. Tolliver gave an indulgent little laugh. "I'm afraid that Annabelle was never very maternal. Like me. I was never very maternal, either. But when Annabelle was a child, things were easier. My husband was alive then, and we were able to afford a nanny for Annabelle. I had help in the house as well. Things were easier."

"Did your son-in-law know that Annabelle was having an affair with this man . . . the riding instructor?"

Mrs. Tolliver looked embarrassed, as though Phoebe had deliberately offended her. She looked away, toying with a china shepherdess that stood upon the mantelpiece. "I . . . I didn't ask him that. But . . . you know Annabelle, Phoebe. She was always . . ."

She hesitated, and I waited with interest. How does a mother describe her only daughter who is, by all accounts, a nymphomaniac?

". . . attractive. Full of life. Leslie was in London all the time. They didn't see a great deal of each other."

"So he didn't know," said Phoebe bluntly. "Or perhaps he just suspected."

"Yes. Perhaps he just suspected."

"Well," said Phoebe, coming to the point. "So what is now going to happen to Charlotte?"

Mrs. Tolliver set the china figure down neatly, exactly, in its customary position. She looked back at Phoebe and her mouth was trembling, but whether with incipient tears or indignation, I could not tell.

"He doesn't want Charlotte back. He said that she's not his child and she's never been his child, and now that Annabelle has left him, he intends washing his hands of Charlotte."

"But he can't do that," said Phoebe, her hackles rising at the very suggestion of such behaviour.

"I don't know whether he can or not. I don't know what to do."

"Then she must be with her mother. Annabelle must take her to South Africa."

"I . . . I don't think that Annabelle will want her."

The enormity of this silenced both Phoebe and myself. We stared, unbelieving, at Mrs. Tolliver, and a flush crept up her neck.

At last Phoebe said bluntly, "You mean that Charlotte would get in Annabelle's way."

"I don't know. Annabelle . . ." I waited for her to tell us next that Annabelle had no more fondness for Charlotte than Leslie Collis had. But Mrs. Tolliver could not bring herself to come out with this. "I don't know what I'm trying to say. I feel torn in all directions. I'm sorry for the child —but, Phoebe, I cannot have her here. I'm too old. This isn't a house for a child. I haven't got a nursery, I haven't even got any toys. Annabelle's dollhouse went years ago, and I gave all her children's books to the hospital."

I thought, *No wonder Charlotte loved the carousel.*

"And I have a life of my own. My own commitments, my friends. It isn't as though she seems particularly happy here. She mopes around most of the time, without saying or doing anything. I admit, I find her difficult. And Betty Curnow only comes in in the mornings. It isn't as though I have good help. I . . . I don't know which way to turn. I'm at my wit's end."

Tears had never been far away. Now, at the end of her tether, she lost control. The tears of older women are ugly. Perhaps ashamed of them or wishing to spare us embarrassment, she turned from the fireplace and took herself over to the long window, where she stood, her back to us, as though admiring her own garden. There came the sound of painful sobs.

I knew that I was very much in the way and

longed for escape. I looked beseechingly in Phoebe's direction and caught her eye.

Phoebe said instantly, "You know, I think a nice hot cup of coffee would do us all good."

Mrs. Tolliver did not turn, but presently in a choked voice she said pathetically, "There's no one to get it. I sent Betty Curnow and Charlotte up to the village. Charlotte wanted to buy some Coca-Cola. We've . . . we've run out. And it seemed a good excuse to get her out of the house. I didn't want her here while I spoke to you . . ."

I said, "I can get coffee."

Mrs. Tolliver blew her nose. This seemed to help a bit. Slightly recovered, she looked at me over her shoulder. Her face was blurred and swollen. "You won't know where to find anything."

"I can look. If you don't mind me going into your kitchen."

"No. Not at all. How kind . . ."

I left them. Let myself quietly out of the drawing room and shut the door and leaned against it, like people do in films. I couldn't like Mrs. Tolliver, but it was impossible not to feel dreadfully sorry for her. Her well-organised existence seemed to be collapsing about her head. Annabelle was, after all, her only child. Now Annabelle's marriage had come to pieces and she was off with her new love to the other end of the world, abandoning both her children and all her responsibilities.

And yet I knew that the bitterest blow of all to the pride of a woman like Mrs. Tolliver was the shaming revelation that Charlotte was not Leslie Collis's child but the unfortunate result of one of Annabelle's many love affairs.

I wondered if she had any idea which love affair it was. For all our sakes, I hoped not.

And Charlotte. *That little face.* I couldn't think about Charlotte. I pulled myself away from the door and went in search of Mrs. Tolliver's kitchen.

By a process of trial and error, opening cupboard doors and pulling out random drawers, I finally assimilated a tray, cups and saucers, a sugar bowl, some spoons. I filled the electric kettle and found a jar of instant coffee. I decided that we could do without biscuits. When the kettle had boiled, I filled the three cups and carried the tray back to the drawing room.

They were still at it, but Mrs. Tolliver, in my absence, seemed to have stopped crying and pulled herself together. Now she sat in a wide-lapped Victorian chair, facing Phoebe.

". . . Perhaps," Phoebe was saying, "your son-in-law will have second thoughts about Charlotte. After all, she has a brother, and it's always been considered very wrong to split up families."

"But Michael is so much older than Charlotte. So much more mature. I don't believe they've ever had very much in common . . ."

She looked up as I appeared through the door, and at once a polite smile turned up the corners of her mouth. She was a lady to whom social graces came automatically, even in times of stress.

"How kind, Prue. So clever." I set down the tray on a low stool. "Oh," a small frown creased her brow. "You've used the best teacups."

"I'm sorry. They were the first I found."

"Oh. Well, never mind. It won't matter for once."

I handed Phoebe her coffee. She took it and stirred it thoughtfully. I sat down, too, and for a moment there was silence, broken only by the tinkling of stirring teaspoons, as though we were gathered together for an enjoyable occasion.

Phoebe broke this silence. "In my opinion," she said, "I think there can be no question of Charlotte returning home. At least until things have simmered down and your son-in-law has had time to sort himself out."

"But her school."

"Don't send her back to that school. I don't like the sound of it, with the boiler blowing that way. It must be very inefficiently administrated. She's far too young for boarding school, anyway, and there can be no point in her returning there if her home life is in pieces. Enough to give any child a nervous breakdown." She sat with her cup and saucer in her lap and looked long and hard at Mrs. Tolliver. "You have to be very careful. You don't want the responsibility of Charlotte, and I can understand that, but for the moment, as far as I can see, you've got it. A life in your hands. A young, sensitive life. She is going to be hurt enough when she knows about her mother. Let us all see that she is not hurt any more than she has to be."

Mrs. Tolliver started to say something, but Phoebe, with unusual bluntness, overrode her.

"I said, I understand your situation. Things are going to be very difficult. For that reason I think it would be much better if you were here on your own, without Charlotte around the place, listening to talk and possibly overhearing telephone calls which she should not. She's an intelligent child, and she'll know instinctively that something is wrong. So I suggest that you simply tell her she's coming to live with me for a little while."

Oh, darling Phoebe. Oh, blessed Phoebe.

"I know I'm a bit of a crock just now, but Prue's with me for another ten days and Lily Tonkins is always a tower of strength in times of emergency."

"But, Phoebe, that's too much."

"I'm very fond of Charlotte. We shall get along very well."

"I know that. And I know that she is devoted to you. But . . . oh, don't think I'm not grateful . . . it will seem so strange to everybody. Leaving me, her grandmother, and coming to stay with you. What will people think? What will they say? This is a small village, and you know both Lily Tonkins and Betty Curnow will talk."

"Yes, they will talk. People always talk. But all the talk in the world is better than having that child hurt any more. Besides," Phoebe said as she set down her empty coffee cup, "we've both got broad shoulders, and," she gave a little chuckle, "let's face it, surely we're getting a bit long in the tooth for a scrap of gossip to bother us. So what do you say?"

Mrs. Tolliver, with obvious relief, finally succumbed.

"I don't mind admitting it would make things very, very much easier for me."

"Will you be in touch with your son-in-law again?"

"Yes. I said I would ring him up tonight. Yesterday evening we were both of us getting a little too emotional. I think he'd probably had far too much to drink. Not that I blame him for that, but neither of us was making much sense."

"In that case you can tell him that Charlotte's coming to stay at Holly Cottage for a little. And you can tell him as well that she's not going back to that boarding school. Perhaps we could get her into the local school here. You could talk it over with him."

"Yes. Yes, I'll do that."

"That's settled, then." Phoebe stood up. "Now Charlotte has already arranged to come to Holly Cottage this morning. Prue is taking her on a picnic. Pack a bag and let her bring that with her. But don't say anything to the child about her mother."

"But she'll have to be told."

"You are family, far too close, too involved. I shall tell her."

For a moment I thought that Mrs. Tolliver was going to object to this. She took a breath to say something but then met Phoebe's eye and didn't say it after all.

"Very well, Phoebe."

"It will be easier if I tell her. For all of us."

At the same snail's pace we trundled homewards. Down the drive of White Lodge, through the gates, past the oak copse. We turned the corner by the church, and the road to home sloped down and away from us, and we could see the whole long blue lake that was the estuary, the floodwaters dazzling with sun pennies.

"Prue, stop the car for a moment."

I did as she said, drawing the car in to the side of the road and switching off the engine. For a little we sat like two aimless tourists, gazing at the familiar view as though we had never seen it before. On the far shore, the gentle hills, patchworked in small fields, drowsed in the morning's warmth. A red tractor, minimised by distance to toy size, was out ploughing, drawing in its wake a flock of screaming white gulls.

At the end of the road, in the lee of the shore, Holly Cottage waited for us, hidden beyond the crest of the hill, slumbering in the sheltered sunshine. But here on the brow of the slope, the sea breezes were never still. Now the thin wind flattened the pale grasses in the roadside ditches and blew the first of the leaves from the topmost branches of the trees that bordered the ancient churchyard.

"So peaceful," said Phoebe, sounding as though she were thinking aloud. "You'd think that here, the end of the world, you'd be safe. I thought so, when I first came to live here with Chips. I thought I'd escaped. But there is no way you can escape reality. Cruelty, indifference, self-ishness."

"All those things are part of people, and people are everywhere."

"Destroying." Phoebe thought this over for a bit, and then said in a changed voice, "Poor woman."

"Mrs. Tolliver. Yes, I'm sorry for her, too. But still, I wonder why she chose to confide in *you*."

"Oh, my dear, it's obvious. She knows I'm an old sinner. She'll never forget that Chips and I lived in happy sin for years. She could talk to me, where she could never have confided in her other friends. Colonel Danby's wife, or the bank man-ager's widow from Porthkerris—they'd have been appalled. And, of course, what's hurting most of all is her pride."

"I thought that, too. But you were marvellous. You always are marvellous, but this morning you were more marvellous than usual."

"I don't know about that."

"I just hope you haven't bitten off more than you can chew. Supposing Leslie Collis really does refuse to have anything more to do with Charlotte; you'll be landed with her indefinitely."

"I wouldn't mind."

"But Phoebe . . ." I stopped, because you can't say to a person you love, You're too old, even if you think that she is.

"You think I'm too old?"

"Other things, too. You've as much a life of your own as Mrs. Tolliver. Why should you be the one who gives it all up? And let's face it, we're all getting older. Even I'm getting older . . ."

"I'm sixty-three. If I manage to stay alive and kicking for another ten years, I shall still be only seventy-three. That's a young woman when you think of Picasso or Arthur Rubenstein."

"What have they got to do with it?"

"And by then Charlotte will be twenty and well able to take care of herself. I really don't see that that's much of a problem."

The windscreen of the Volkswagen was dirty. I found in some pocket a grubby rag and began to try in a desultory sort of way to clean the glass.

I said, "When I was in the kitchen getting the coffee, did she make any reference to Daniel?"

"None."

"You didn't say anything?"

"Heaven forbid."

I was making the smears on the windscreen, if anything, worse. I stuffed the rag back into its hiding place.

"He's coming here, you know, this morning, for the picnic. I offered to fetch him in the car, but he said he'd make his own way."

"That's just as well."

I looked at her. "You're going to tell Daniel about all this?"

"Of course I shall tell him. I shall tell him everything. Three heads are better than two, and I'm sick and tired of all of us keeping secrets from each other. Perhaps if we hadn't kept secrets, none of this would have happened."

"Oh, Phoebe, I hardly think so."

"Maybe you're right. But let's start being completely frank and truthful; then we'll all know where we stand. Besides, Daniel has a right to know."

"What do you think he'll do?"

"*Do?*" Phoebe gazed at me blankly. "Why should he do anything?"

"He's Charlotte's father."

"Leslie Collis is Charlotte's father."

It was just what I had said to Daniel, sitting with him by the pretend fire; trying to be down-to-earth and sensible, jollying him along. But surely, now, things were taking a different course.

"He may not *be* responsible," I pointed out, "but that's not going to stop him feeling that way."

"And what do you imagine he's going to do about it?"

"I don't know."

"In that case, I can tell you. Nothing. Because there is nothing that he can do. And because even if there were, he wouldn't do it."

"How do you know?"

"Because I know Daniel."

"I know him, too."

"I only wish you did."

"What's that supposed to mean?"

Phoebe sighed. "Oh, nothing. It's just that I'm afraid you've fallen in love with him."

Her voice, as always, was inconsequential, as though she were talking of something of no importance. As a result, I was taken unawares. I said, trying to sound as casual as she did, "I don't think I know what falling in love actually means. It's always been a sort of nonword with me. Like 'forgive.' I never understand the word 'forgive.' If you don't forgive, then you're mean and resentful and grudge-bearing; and if you do, then you're smug and sanctimonious."

But Phoebe would not be waylaid into this interesting discussion. She stuck to her point.

"Well, 'love,' then. Perhaps that's an easier word to define."

"If you want definitions, then I feel as though I've known him always. I feel as though already we've shared a past. And I don't want to lose him, because I think we need each other."

"Did you feel this way before he unfolded to you the great saga of Annabelle?"

"I think so. Yes. So you see I'm not just feeling sorry for him."

"Why should you be sorry for him? He has everything—youth, a terrifying talent, and now fame and money and all the material things that go with them."

"But how can you discount what happened between Daniel and Annabelle? He's felt guilty for eleven years because he didn't even know if the child was his or not. Wouldn't you feel sorry for any man who had that load of guilt on his back for eleven years?"

"The guilt was of his own making. And he didn't need to run away."

"Perhaps he didn't run away. Perhaps he did what Chips told him to do, which was the only possible, reasonable thing."

"Did he speak about this to you?"

"Yes. And he asked me to go to Greece with him. To Spetsai. That was before he told me about Annabelle and Charlotte. But afterwards we talked about it again, and he said that it wouldn't be any good, because he couldn't go on running away from the inside of his own head."

"Would you have gone? To Greece?"

"Yes."

"And afterwards?"

"I don't know."

"That's not good enough for you, Prue."

"You sound like my mother."

"At the risk of sounding like your mother— who, incidentally, is nobody's fool—I have to say it. You don't know Daniel. He is a true artist: impermanent, restless, impractical."

"I know he's impractical." I smiled. "He told me once that he had a car, and at the end of three years he'd only just learned how to work the heater."

But Phoebe ignored my small attempt at humour and went on doggedly.

"He's unreliable, too, because he's always lost

in his own form of creation. It makes him, in a way, negative. Maddening."

"Oh, come off it, Phoebe, you know you adore him."

"I do, Prue, I do. But face him with day-to-day decisions and responsibilities, and I could never truly predict how he would react."

"Are you talking about Daniel as a prospective husband?"

"I wouldn't intrude that far."

"You knew him when he was twenty. You can't judge him by the person he was eleven years ago. He's a man now."

"Yes, I know that. And people mature, of course. But do their personalities change so much? You're such a special person, Prue, I wouldn't want you ever to be hurt. And Daniel could hurt you. Not deliberately, but by the sins of omission. His work fills his life, and I don't know how much room there is left over for personal things like loving people and being with them, and taking care of them."

"Perhaps I could take care of him."

"Yes, perhaps you could, for a little while. But I think not indefinitely. I don't see how it could be possible to stay forever with a man who I knew was afraid of permanency, emotional involvements, becoming trapped."

It was no good arguing with her. I sat saying nothing, gazing ahead of me through the dusty windscreen and seeing nothing. The funny thing was that we both seemed to be on the same side. She put out her hand and laid it over mine. Her fingers were warm, but I could feel the cold, hard pressure of her bulky, old-fashioned rings.

"Don't create fantasies about Daniel. They will probably never come true. And if you expect nothing of him, you will at least never be disappointed."

I was thinking of Charlotte. "I don't believe he will run away from this."

"And I believe that he has no alternative. Perhaps you should run away, too. Go back to London. Get your life in perspective. Ring up that nice young man who brought you the dead chrysanthemums."

"Oh, *Phoebe.*" It took a small effort even to remember his name. "They weren't dead when he gave them to me."

"When you see him again, you may feel quite differently about him."

"No. I shan't do that. Anyway, he doesn't

make me laugh." Nigel Gordon. I knew that now I should probably never get to go to Scotland.

"Well, you must make up your own mind." She gave my hand a pat and then sat back in her seat with her hands in her lap. "I've said it. Interfered. Cleared my muddy conscience. Now perhaps we'd better go home and break the news about Charlotte coming to stay to Lily Tonkins. If anything's going to stop her singing "Guard Us Oh Thou Great Jehovah," then that is. On the other hand, she always enjoys a drama, so maybe she'll take it quite well. As well, Charlotte will be turning up at Holly Cottage at any moment, and we've got the picnic to organise, as if life wasn't already sufficiently complicated."

I had forgotten the picnic. Now, starting the engine and letting off the brake, I wished that Phoebe had not found it necessary to remind me.

"Well, I don't know," said Lily when we told her about Charlotte coming to stay. "Leaving her granny and coming here. Seems funny." She looked from Phoebe's innocent face to mine. I hastily smiled, brightly and blankly. "I suppose, come to think of it, it's not all that surprising. The child's here most of the time whenever she's meant to be staying with Mrs. Tolliver. Just as easy to make up a bed and be done with it.''

Phoebe looked relieved. "You are good, Lily. And I hope it won't be too much extra work. I know you've got enough to do as it is just now, but once my arm's out of this dratted cast . . .''

"Don't you worry, Miss Shackleton, we'll manage lovely. Any road, she's no trouble. Quiet little soul. Doesn't even eat much.'' She moved her eyes once more from Phoebe's face to mine. She frowned. "There's nothing *wrong*, is there?''

There was a small pause. Then Phoebe said, "No. Not really. But Mrs. Tolliver finds it . . . awkward having Charlotte living at White Lodge. I don't think they find it too easy to get on together, and we all decided it might be better if she came here for a bit.''

"Well, certainly more fun for her," Lily pointed out. "Betty Curnow's a nice enough person, but she was never much of a one for fun. Miss La-di-dah we used to call her when we were all at school together, and marrying up with a sanitary inspector didn't make her any more free and easy.''

"Yes. Well, maybe Joshua Curnow isn't the jolliest of men, but I'm sure he's made Betty a marvellous husband," said Phoebe soothingly before bringing Lily back to the matter at hand. "Where do you think Charlotte should sleep?"

"We'll put her in Mr. Armitage's old dressing room. The bed's made up; just needs a bit of an airing."

"And the picnic, don't forget. They're all going on a picnic."

"That's right. Ham sandwiches I've made, and a little salad in a plastic box. And there's chocolate cake with orange icing . . ."

"How delicious. I wish I were going . . . my favourite . . . what a lovely picnic . . ." And Phoebe took herself off upstairs to divest herself of her poncho and change her shoes. We heard her footsteps cross the floorboards above us.

I said, "You are a tower of strength, Lily. That's what Phoebe always says about you."

"Get away," said Lily, pleased.

"I can help you. Give me something to do to help you."

"You can string beans for dinner tonight. One thing I can't abide is stringing beans. Give me a carrot to peel or a turnip and I'm happy as a sandboy. But fiddley old beans I can't abide . . ."

So I was in the garden, in the sunshine, in one of Phoebe's rickety old garden chairs, stringing beans, when Charlotte finally arrived. I heard the sound of a car and laid down the knife and the basket and went through to the front of the house, only to find both Phoebe and Lily there before me. Betty Curnow had brought Charlotte, driving Mrs. Tolliver's car. Charlotte was already out of it, and Lily had opened the boot and was lifting out her suitcase. Charlotte wore her grey flannel coat, with her red handbag slung across one shoulder. Her travelling clothes. I wondered how she had felt, putting them on; dressing herself for another journey, another house; shunted from pillar to post because nobody wanted her, nobody could be bothered to take care of her.

"Hello, Charlotte."

She turned and saw me. "Hello." She was very pale, unsmiling. Her spectacles were crooked. Her hair looked greasy, as though in need of a good wash, and somebody—perhaps Charlotte herself —had parted it carelessly and pinned back the front lock with a blue plastic slide.

"This is fun. Do you want to come upstairs and look at your bedroom?"

"All right."

Lily and Phoebe were engaged in conversation with Betty Curnow, so I took the suitcase, and we started together towards the front door. But then Charlotte remembered her manners and stopped.

"Thank you very much, Mrs. Curnow, for bringing me."

"That's all right, love," said Betty Curnow. "See and be a good girl, now."

We went upstairs. The little room that had been Chips's dressing room was next to mine. Lily had been through it like a dose of salts, and it smelt strongly of polish and clean, starched linen. Phoebe had found time to pick flowers for the dressing table, and the open window framed the same view that I enjoyed, of the garden and the escallonia hedge and the flood tide of the estuary beyond.

The room was so small and delightful, so exactly the right size and shape for a little girl, that I expected a spark of enthusiasm. But Charlotte seemed unseeing; her expression showed nothing.

I set down her suitcase. "Do you want to unpack now, or later?"

"If I could just get Teddy out."

Teddy, flattened, was on the top of the suitcase. She lifted him out and set him on her pillow.

"What about everything else?"

"It doesn't matter. I'll do it later."

"Well . . . if you'd like to take off your coat,

you can come down to the garden and help me. I'm stringing beans for Lily Tonkins and I could do with a bit of help."

She took off her red shoulder bag and laid it on her dressing table, then unbuttoned her grey flannel coat. I found a hanger and put it away in the wardrobe. Under the coat she wore a blue T-shirt and a faded cotton skirt.

"Do you need a sweater?"

"No. I'm all right."

We made our way downstairs again. In the chest in the hall I found an old car rug, in the kitchen took a second knife from the drawer. We went back out into the garden. I spread the rug and we sat on it together, with the basket of beans and Lily's largest saucepan between us.

"The knives are very sharp. You'll be careful not to cut yourself?"

"I've strung beans heaps of times."

Pause.

"Isn't it a lovely day? You haven't forgotten about our picnic, have you?"

"No."

"Daniel's definitely coming. He'll be here any moment now. He said he'd try and get a lift over from Porthkerris."

Pause.

"I wanted Phoebe to come with us to Penjizal, but she said that she was frightened that the wind would blow her over the edge of the cliff. Did you remember to bring the Coca-Cola?"

"Yes. Mrs. Curnow said she'd give it to Lily."

"Lily's made us ham sandwiches, just the kind you wanted. And a chocolate cake . . ."

Charlotte looked at me. "You don't have to cheer me up, you know."

I felt, and with some reason, extremely foolish. I said, "I'm sorry."

She went back clumsily to slicing her bean.

"Charlotte . . . didn't you want to come and stay with Phoebe?"

"I've never stayed before."

"I . . . I don't know what you're trying to say."

"Something's happened. And nobody wants to tell me."

I was apprehensive. "What makes you say that?"

She did not reply, but a movement behind me caught her eye and she looked up, over my shoulder. I turned and saw Phoebe emerging through the garden door. She still wore her hat but had abandoned the gaudy poncho, and now her knotted scarf fluttered in the breeze like a little flag, and the sunlight winked back at us from the gold chains slung about her neck. She lugged, in her good arm, a deck chair, and I got up and went to take it from her and set it up by the rug where we sat. She sank into it, her knees jutting beneath the folk weave of her skirt.

There seemed no point in prevaricating. I caught and held her eye. "Charlotte and I were just talking." Phoebe's gaze was calm and untroubled. I knew that she understood. I settled down on the rung once more and picked up my knife. "She's wondering why she's here."

"Mostly," Phoebe told her, "because we want you."

"Mummy's not coming back from Majorca, is she?"

"Why do you say that?"

"She isn't coming, is she?"

"No," said Phoebe.

I selected a bean and began, very neatly, to string and slice it.

"I knew," said Charlotte.

"Would you like to tell us how you knew?"

"Because she had this friend. He was called Desmond. He used to come and see her. He had a riding school quite near our house in Sunningdale. They used to go riding together, and then he'd come back and have a drink or something. He was called Desmond. She went to Majorca with him."

"How do you know that?"

"Because there was one night at the end of the holidays. Before I went back to school and the boiler blew up. Daddy was in Brussels on business. And I had to get up in the middle of the night to go to the bathroom, and then I was thirsty, and I thought I'd go downstairs and get some Coke out of the fridge. I'm not meant to, but I do sometimes. And then when I was halfway down the stairs I heard voices. I heard a man talking and I thought perhaps it was a burglar. I thought perhaps it was a burglar and he was going to shoot Mummy. But then he said something and I knew it was Desmond. So I sat on the stairs and listened. And they were talking about Majorca. She told Daddy she was going on holiday with an old school friend. I heard her telling him at breakfast one morning, but I knew she was going with Desmond."

"Did you say anything?"

"No. Daddy never listens to me anyway, and I was frightened."

"Frightened of your father?"

"No. Just frightened. Frightened of her going and never coming back."

"Did you know that your father rang your grandmother last night?"

"I wasn't asleep. I heard the phone ringing. Granny's drawing room is under my bedroom. You can hear people talking, but you can't hear what they say. But I did hear her say his name. He's called Leslie. And I knew it was him. And I thought perhaps he'd just rung up to see how I was. But this morning everything felt so horrible, I knew it hadn't just been that. And Granny was all funny and cross, and then she sent me and Betty Curnow up to the village to buy Coke. So I knew something was wrong, because I'm always allowed to go to the village by myself."

"I think your grandmother didn't want you to overhear. To be distressed."

"And then when we got back again, Mrs. Curnow and me, Granny said I was coming to stay with you."

"I hope you were pleased."

All the time that she had been speaking, Charlotte had sat with downcast eyes, fiddling with a runner bean that she had slowly and deliberately torn to shreds. Now she looked up at Phoebe, her eyes anxious behind the lenses of her unbecoming spectacles. She was being very brave. "She isn't ever coming back, is she?"

"No. She's going to go and live in South Africa."

"What will happen to us? To Michael and me? Daddy can't look after us. At least, he wouldn't mind looking after Michael. They're always doing things together, like going shooting and watching rugger matches and things like that. But he wouldn't want to look after me."

"Maybe not," said Phoebe. "But I would. That's why I asked your grandmother if I could have you to stay with me."

"But not *forever?*"

"Nothing is ever forever."

"Won't I ever see Daddy and Michael again?"

"Yes, of course you will. After all, Michael is your brother."

Charlotte screwed up her nose. "He's not always very kind. I don't like him that much."

"Even so, he is your brother. Perhaps, next holidays, he'd like to come and stay with me as well. But I expect your grandmother might like to have him."

"She didn't want me," Charlotte pointed out.

"You mustn't think that. She just doesn't find it very easy to have a person of your age around the place. It's called not being good with children. Lots of the nicest people are like that."

"You're good with children," Charlotte told her.

"That's because I like them." Phoebe smiled. "Particularly you. That's why, for the time being at any rate, I want you to stay here."

"What about my school?" Charlotte was still being very wary. "I have to go back to school at the end of the week."

"I had a word with your grandmother about that. Do you like your boarding school?"

"No, I hate it. I hate having to be away all the time. And I'm much the youngest; there's nobody younger than me, not boarding. There are day girls, but they're all friends and they do things together at the weekend, and they don't want me. I wanted to be a day girl, too, but Mummy said it was much better to be a boarder. I don't know why it should be better. I thought it was horribler."

"Then you wouldn't mind too much if you didn't go back?"

Cautiously, Charlotte considered this. For the first time a gleam of something hopeful crossed her face. "Why? Don't I have to?"

"No, I don't think you do. If you're going to

live with me, then it would be much easier for all of us if you went to our local school. Nobody's a boarder there, and I think you'd enjoy it."

"I'm not very good at lessons."

"People can't be good at everything. You're good at drawing and making things. And if you like music, they have a very good music master, and they have a proper orchestra and give concerts. I know one boy, he's only your age, and he plays the clarinet."

"Could I go there?"

"If you wanted, I think it could be arranged."

"I do want it."

"Then you'll stay with me?"

"You mean . . . never go back to Daddy?"

"Yes," said Phoebe gently. "Perhaps that is what I mean."

"But . . . you just said . . . you said nothing is ever forever." Her eyes were filling with tears, and it was almost too painful to watch. "I can't stay with you . . ."

"Yes you can. For as long as you, like. So you see, although the worst has happened, the world hasn't come to an end. You can talk about things, to Prue and to me. You haven't got to keep everything to yourself any longer. Don't go on trying to be brave. It doesn't matter about crying . . ."

It was a dam burst of tears, uncontrollable. Charlotte's mouth went square in the manner of all weeping children, but the sobs that racked her small frame sounded more like the suffering grief of an adult.

"Oh, Charlotte . . ."

Phoebe leaned forward in her chair, her arms— the good arm, and the stiff one in its plaster cast —outflung, an open invitation to comfort and love. At any other time the effect of this typically expansive gesture might have been comic, but it wasn't funny now. ". . . come away, my darling."

And Charlotte scrambled to her feet and flung herself into the lopsided embrace, winding her arms tightly around Phoebe's neck, burying her face in Phoebe's shoulder, knocking Phoebe's hat askew.

I picked up the beans and the saucepan and went indoors. Because it was their own private moment. Because she was Daniel's child. And because I thought I might be going to cry as well.

The kitchen was empty. Through the open back door I could see Lily out on the drying green, pegging out a line of snowy tea towels. Now she was onto another hymn.

Do no sinful action
Speak no angry wer-erd.

I put the beans and the saucepan down on the end of the scrubbed pine table and went upstairs to my bedroom. I had made my bed this morning, but since then Lily had been what she called through the room, which meant a strong smell of floor polish and everything on my dressing table arranged in a straight line. I sat on the edge of the bed and after a little realized that I wasn't going to cry after all. But I felt drained, disoriented, as though I had spent the last three hours in a dark cinema, absorbed in some deeply emotional film, and was now back in the street again, dazzled by the light, blundering my way along an unfamiliar pavement; incapable.

Mummy's not coming back from Majorca, is she? Daddy never listens to me anyway. He wouldn't want to look after me. I wanted to be a day girl, but Mummy said it was much better to be a boarder. My grandmother doesn't want me.

Oh, dear Lord, the things we do to our children.

The window was open, the curtains stirring in the warm breeze. I got off the bed and went to the window and leaned out of it, my elbows on the sill. Below me on the grass, Phoebe and Charlotte still sat. The tears seemed to be over, and now all that could be heard was the companionable murmur of their conversation. Charlotte was back on the rug again, cross-legged, absorbed in making a daisy chain. I looked down at her bowed head, the vulnerable back of her neck. I remembered being her age. My parents were divorced and I lived with my mother, but never was I unloved, unwanted, shunted off to boarding schools. I remembered travelling to Northumberland to stay with my father, willing the train to travel faster and faster as we rocketed north. I remembered being met by him at Newcastle Station and racing up the platform to be swept into his sturdy, tweed-smelling embrace.

I remembered my mother's little house in London, the bedroom she decorated for me exactly the way I wanted it. The clothes she bought me, which were the clothes that I was allowed to choose for myself. The fun of dancing classes in the winter, and Christmas parties; being taken to the pantomime at the Palladium and the *Sleeping Beauty* at Covent Garden.

I remembered shopping in Harrod's, the tedium of buying school clothes rewarded by the treat of a chocolate milk shake at the soda fountain. And summer outings down the Thames, by boat, with a party of small friends and all the shivery anticipation of a visit to the Tower of London.

And always Cornwall, and Penmarron. And Phoebe.

Oh, my darling, how lovely to see you again.

Phoebe. I was suddenly filled with nameless apprehensions for her. What had she taken on, so impulsively, so lovingly? She was sixty-three and had already fallen from a worm-ridden chair and broken her arm. Supposing she had not simply broken her arm, but her hip, or her neck? Supposing she had struck her head and lain there, on the studio floor, concussed, with nobody knowing or coming to look for her? My imagination turned and fled but immediately came up with alternative and even more horrendous fabrications.

I thought of Phoebe driving her old car. She had never done this with much concentration, since she was always being diverted by the goings-on in the roads and streets down which she trundled, quite often on the wrong side of the white line, believing that provided she continued to blow the horn, nothing too dreadful could happen.

Supposing she had a heart attack and died? It happened to other people; why should it not happen to Phoebe? Supposing one summer day she went swimming from the old seawall, as she liked to do. Supposing she dived, wearing her old-fashioned bathing suit and her plastic bath hat, and never came up again? There seemed no end to the possible fatalities, and if anything happened to Phoebe, then who would take care of Charlotte? Once more my mind scurried ahead, searching for a solution to this hypothetical problem.

Who would have her? Myself? In a basement flat in Islington? My mother? Or perhaps my father? He was the sort of man who would take in any lame dog. I tried to picture Charlotte at Windyedge, but somehow nothing quite fit. My young stepmother would welcome any child who would ride her horses, muck out stables, clean tack, and go hunting, but she would have little in common with a small girl who only wanted to play the clarinet and draw.

These gloomy thoughts might have gone on forever, but at that moment I was brought back to reality by the sound of the morning train from Porthkerris, rattling through the cutting behind the house. It appeared busily around the curve of the single line to draw up at the halt, looking like a toy train, the kind that is wound up with a key. For a moment it stood there, and then somebody blew a whistle and waved a green flag, and it moved on, pulling away from the station and leaving behind it on the empty platform a single, lonely figure.

Daniel. Come for the picnic.

As soon as it was clear, he jumped down onto the line, crossed it, climbed a fence, and started down the track, past the small anchorage where the sailing boats bobbed at high tide and so onto the old seawall. He wore blue jeans, a navy blue sweater, a white canvas smock.

I watched his approach, ambling long-legged, his hands in his pockets, and longed for him to be the sort of person to whom I could run with all my problems, just as I used to run into the arms of my father on Newcastle Station. I wanted to be embraced, reassured, loved. I wanted to gabble out to him everything that had occurred on that endless morning, and to be told that nothing mattered, I was never to worry again, he would deal with everything . . .

But Phoebe, who loved Daniel, was wiser than I.

Face him with day-to-day decisions and responsibilities and I could never truly predict how he would react.

I didn't want him to be that sort of person. I wanted him to take charge. To have taken charge.

I watched him coming and knew that if what was happening to us all were a story I was making up, then this moment would be the beginning of the end. He would have everything solved, decisions taken and plans formed. I devised a film, slow motion, soft focus: Daniel coming through the gate in the escallonia hedge to run in floating strides up the slope of the lawn. To embrace Phoebe, scoop his child up into his arms, call me down from my open window in order to plan our future together. Violins would soar. "The End" would appear upon the screen. Credits would roll and we would all live happily ever after.

Don't create fantasies about Daniel. They will probably never come true. Instead, reality. Phoebe would take him aside, relate to him bluntly what had happened. No more secrets, Daniel. Annabelle has taken off and nobody else wants Charlotte. Nobody else wants your daughter.

And he? What would he do? I did not want to think about it. I did not want to know what was going to happen next.

He had moved out of sight, hidden from my view by the slope of the bank and the height of the hedge. I closed my window and turned back to my room. In the mirror over my dressing table I caught sight of my reflection, and my appearance was so appalling that I spent the next five minutes doing things to improve it. Washed my face with a scalding-hot flannel, scrubbed my nails with Phoebe's lavender-scented soap, brushed and combed my hair. I took a fresh cotton shirt from a drawer, changed my shoes, applied mascara, sprayed scent.

"Prue!" Charlotte's voice.

"I'm here. In my bedroom."

"Can I come in?" The door opened, and her face appeared around the edge of it. "Daniel's here."

"I saw him get off the train."

"But Phoebe's taken him down to the studio. She says she wants to show him something that belonged to Chips. She says they'll be about ten minutes. What a lovely smell!"

"It's Dior. I always use it. Want a squirt?"

"Don't you mind?"

"Don't take it all."

She sprayed on some scent, breathing in the perfume with an ecstatic expression on her face. I picked up my comb and tidied her hair for her, straightening the parting and refastening the plastic slide.

When this was done, I said, "Perhaps we should go down to the kitchen and start packing our picnic basket. And it might be a good idea if you found your Wellingtons and an anorak."

"But it won't rain today."

"This is Cornwall . . . you never know what it's going to do."

So we were in the kitchen when Phoebe eventually came to find us. I saw her through the window, walking slowly up the brick path that led from the walled garden and the studio. She came towards us like an old person. She was alone. She came through the garden door and saw us standing, waiting for her. She told us that Daniel had gone. He would not, after all, be able to come with us on the picnic. He was sorry.

"But he promised . . ." Charlotte kept saying, near to tears. "He *said* he'd come . . ."

Phoebe would not meet my eyes.

So we never got to go to Penjizal. Somehow, by then, none of us had the heart to go anywhere. We ate the picnic right there, in the garden of Holly Cottage. We never saw the seals.

It was evening before I got Phoebe to myself. Charlotte was engrossed in television, and I cornered my aunt by the sink.

"Why did he go?"

"I warned you," said Phoebe.

"Where did he go?"

"I've no idea. Back to Porthkerris, I suppose."

I said, "I'm going to take the car. I'm going to go and see him."

"Don't do that."

"Why not? You can't stop me."

"Ring him first, if you must. Talk to him. Make sure that he wants to see you."

I went straight to the telephone. Of course he would want to see me. I dialled the number of the Castle Hotel, and when the girl on the switch-board answered, I asked for Daniel Cassens. But she put me through to the Reception desk, and a girl's voice told me that Mr. Cassens had gone, checked out, and left no forwarding address.

Chapter 7

I WASHED CHARLOTTE'S HAIR and trimmed the ragged ends with Phoebe's sewing scissors. Clean, it was the colour of chestnuts shot through with unexpected copper lights.

Phoebe telephoned the headmaster of the local school and took Charlotte for an interview. She returned home full of excitement. She would have a new uniform, navy-blue and white. They had a pottery wheel in the art room. She was going to learn how to play the clarinet.

We watched, on television, a pretty girl showing us how to make a dolls' house out of cardboard boxes. We took the car into Porthkerris, and went to visit the wine merchant and were given four sturdy crates that had once held bottles of Scotch whisky. We bought a Stanley knife, and little pots of paint and some brushes. We bought tubes of glue. We came home and began to measure and mark out the door, the windows. The kitchen was littered with sheets of newspaper, scraps of card, all the tools of our trade.

Now there was a new moon in the night sky. It hung in the east, a silvery eyelash, and its pale reflection hung in the black waters of the estuary, drowned in trembling slivers of light.

"Prue."

"What is it?"

"Where has Daniel gone?"

"I don't know."

"Why did he go?"

"I don't know that, either."

"Is he ever coming back?"

"I expect he will. One day."

"People always go away. People I like. When Michael first went to school, the house was funny without him. All quiet and empty. And I had a nanny once, when I was very little, about six. I really liked her. But she had to leave and go and look after her mother. And now Daniel's gone."

"You scarcely know Daniel."

"But I've always known about him. Phoebe used to tell me about him. She used to show me bits in the newspaper about him, when he was having exhibitions and things in America. And she used to tell me about him."

"But, still, you scarcely knew him. You only met him for a day or so."

"I didn't want him to go away. It wasn't just the picnic. It wasn't just not seeing the seals. We can do that any time."

"Then what was it?"

"I wanted to tell him things, show him things. I wanted to show him the dolls' house. I wanted to *ask* him things. Daddy never has time to answer properly if you ask him things. And Daniel doesn't talk to you as though you're little, he talks as though you are a grown up person. He'd never tell you that you were being a nuisance or that you were stupid."

"Well . . . perhaps you have a lot in common. You're interested in the same sort of things. Perhaps that's why you feel so close to him."

"I wish he would come back."

"He's a busy man. An important man. And now he's a famous man. He has so many things that he has to do. And an artist is . . . different from other men. He needs to be free. It's hard for someone like Daniel to put down roots, to stay in the same place all the time, and be with the same people."

"Phoebe's an artist, and she stays in the same place."

"Phoebe is different. Phoebe is special."

"I know. That's why I love her. But I love Daniel too."

"You mustn't love him too much, Charlotte."

"Why not?"

"Because it's no good loving a person too much, if you may never see them again . . . oh, don't start to cry. Please don't cry. It's just that it's true, and it's no good either of us pretending that it isn't."

We painted the door red, the frames of the windows black. Lily found an old dress box, and we cut the roof from the lid of this and scored a central line and bent it into a gable. We painted tiles.

One day it rained, and there was a great wind, and Charlotte and I walked over the golf links and down to the beach. There was sand blowing everywhere, and the breakers poured into the shore from half a mile out or more. The rushes on the dunes were flattened by this wind, and the sea gulls abandoned the coast and flew inland to float and scream over fields of newly turned plough.

No letter came for Charlotte, no postcard from South Africa. We learned, through Betty Curnow and Lily Tonkins, that Mrs. Tolliver had gone to spend a few days with a friend at Helford. Which made three people who had run away.

We constructed furniture for the doll's house out of empty matchboxes; we painted wallpaper. We raided Phoebe's rag bag and made carpets from scraps of tweed with fringed ends. Just like real, said Charlotte when we laid them, and she closed the door of the dolls' house and put her face to the window, loving the smallness of everything, the little, safe, miniature world.

One night, "I can't bear to see you looking so unhappy," Phoebe told me, but I pretended that I had not heard her, because I did not want to talk about Daniel.

He was gone. Back to his nomadic, searching, restless life. Back to his painting, his exhibition, Peter Chastal. Perhaps, by now, back to America. Much later, when he felt able, maybe he would send me a postcard. I saw it, dropping through the letter box of my front door in Islington. A brightly coloured picture of the Statue of Liberty, perhaps, or the Golden Gate bridge, or Fujiyama.

Having a wonderful time, wish you were here. Daniel.

There was a future. My future. My job, my flat, my own friends. I would go back to London and pick up the threads again. But on my own, as I had never been alone before.

I had the dream again, the swimming dream. It was the same as before. The water first shallow, and then deep and warm. The racing current. The sensation of being swept along by this flood, not struggling but acquiescent. Not dying, I reminded myself at the end of the dream. Not dying, but loving. So why did I wake with tears wet on my cheeks?

The passing days had lost their names, just as I had lost all sense of their passing. Then suddenly it was a Tuesday and time to be practical. Phoebe had decided the previous evening that I should drive her and Charlotte into Penzance, where we would buy the new navy-and-white school uniform. Perhaps, as a treat, we would have lunch in a restaurant or go down to the harbour and see if the Scilly Islands steamer was in.

But these plans did not come off, because early that morning Lily Tonkins rang to say that Ernest, her husband, had been taken poorly. Phoebe answered the telephone call, and Charlotte and I stood around and listened to the quaking voice over the line.

"Up all night," Lily told Phoebe.

Phoebe said, "Oh, dear."

Lily enlarged on the details. Phoebe's face took on an expression of horror. "Oh, *dear*." After this she hastily agreed that on no account was Lily to abandon her ailing husband until the doctor had seen him. She rang off. Lily was not coming to work today.

We hastily changed our arrangements. I would stay at Holly Cottage to do a bit of sketchy housework and cook the lunch, and Mr. Thomas, in his trusty taxi, would be asked to make the trip into Penzance with Phoebe and Charlotte.

Charlotte was slightly indignant about this.

"I thought we were going to have lunch in a restaurant."

"It wouldn't be any fun without Prue," Phoebe told her briskly. "We'll do it another day, when I have to go and see the bank manager or have my hair done."

A telephone call was duly made, and Mr. Thomas turned up in ten minutes with his chauffeur's hat on his head and the wheels of his car encrusted in pig manure. Phoebe and Charlotte clambered in, and I waved them away and then returned indoors to deal with the morning chores.

They were not very arduous. Lily cleaned the house so thoroughly every day that once I had made the beds, scoured the bath, and cleared the ashes out of the sitting room grate, everything looked more or less as usual. I went into the kitchen, made a cup of coffee and started to peel potatoes. It was a grey, still day, with rain in the air. When I had finished the potatoes, I pulled on a pair of rubber boots and went down to the vegetable garden to cut a cauliflower. As I returned to the house, I heard the sound of a car coming down the road towards the house. I looked at my watch and saw that it was only an hour since Phoebe and Charlotte had set off. There was no way that the shopping expedition could be over so soon.

The car came over the railway bridge, and I knew then that it was heading for Holly Cottage, for we were the last house on the road, and at the end of it lay only the dead end, the padlocked iron gates of the old shipyard.

I hurried back inside. In the kitchen I laid my knife and the cauliflower on the draining board, and then, still wearing Lily's apron and my boots, went through the hall and out the front door.

There, on the gravel, was parked an unfamiliar car. An Alfa-Romeo, long and sleek, dark green and travel-stained. The driver's door was already open, and behind the wheel, his eyes on my face, sat Daniel.

On that still, misty morning, there was little sound. Then, from far away, I heard the scream of some gulls flying low over the empty sands of the estuary. Slowly, he climbed out of the car and straightened himself cautiously, arching his back, and putting up a hand to massage the back of his neck. He was wearing his usual strange assembly of clothes, and there lay the dark shadow of stubble on his chin. He shut the car door behind him, and it closed with a solid expensive-sounding thud. He said my name.

That proved it was true. He wasn't in London. He wasn't in New York. He wasn't in San Francisco. He was here. Back. Home.

I said, "What are you doing?"

"What do you think I'm doing?"

"Who's car is that?"

"Mine." He began to walk stiffly towards me.

"But you hate cars."

"I know, but it's still mine. I bought it yesterday." He reached my side and put his hands on my shoulders and stooped and kissed my cheek, and his chin felt rough and scratchy against my skin. I looked up at him. His face was colourless, grey with tiredness, but his eyes were bright with secret laughter.

"You're wearing Lily's apron."

"Lily's not here. Ernest's ill. You haven't shaved."

"Didn't have time. I left London at three o'clock this morning. Where's Phoebe?"

"She and Charlotte have gone to do some shopping."

"Aren't you going to ask me in?"

"Yes . . . yes, of course. I'm sorry. It's just that you were the last person I expected to see. Come along. I'll make you some coffee, or bacon and eggs if you want something to eat."

"Coffee would be fine."

We went back indoors. The house felt warm after the chilly dampness outside. I led the way through the hall and heard him close the front door behind us. In the kitchen I saw the cauliflower and the knife by the sink where I had left them, and for a moment, so disoriented was I, found myself wondering what I had intended doing with them.

I filled the electric kettle and plugged it in and switched it on. When I turned around, I saw that Daniel had pulled out a chair and was sitting at the head of the long scrubbed pine table. He had an elbow on the table and was rubbing his eyes with his hand, as though it were possible to erase exhaustion.

He said, "I haven't driven so far or so fast in my life, I don't think." He took his hand away and looked up at me, and I had forgotten the darkness of his eyes, the pupils round and dark as black olives. He still looked exhausted, but there was something else about him, an exhilaration, perhaps, that I could not fathom, because I had not seen it in him before.

I said, "What made you buy a car?"

"I wanted to get back to you all, and it seemed the quickest way."

"Have you found out how the heater works?"

It wasn't much of a joke, but it helped break the tension.

He smiled. "Not yet. Like I told you, I've only had it for a day." He crossed his arms on the tabletop. He said, "Phoebe told me, you know. About Annabelle and Leslie Collis and Mrs. Tolliver."

"Yes. I know."

"And Charlotte."

"Yes."

"Was Charlotte disappointed about the picnic?"

"Yes."

"I couldn't stay, Prue. I had to get away. By myself. Do you understand?"

"Where did you go?"

"I went back to Porthkerris. I walked back, over the dunes and along the cliffs. When I got back to the Castle Hotel, I packed my suitcase without any clear idea of what I was going to do next. But then, when it was packed, I picked up the telephone and rang Lewis Falcon. I'd been meaning to get in touch with him ever since I got down here, but somehow with one thing and another I'd never got around to it. He was great. I told him who I was and said that we'd never met. And he said that he knew who I was, because he'd heard about me through Peter Chastal, and why didn't I come out to Lanyon to see him? So I said I'd do that, but what I needed was a bed for a couple of nights, and he said that would be okay too. So I checked out and got a taxi to drive me to Lanyon.

"He's a marvellous man. Immensely likeable, totally uncurious. With him, I found I could switch off; as though I were pulling down a great fireproof safety curtain between myself and everything that Phoebe had told me. The psychoanalyst's seventh veil, perhaps. He showed me his studio, and we looked at his work, and we talked shop as though nothing else existed for either of us.

"That was all right for a couple of days, and then I knew that I had to get back to London. So he drove me to the station and I caught the morning train.

"When I got to London I went to the gallery to see Peter. I was still in this extraordinary state of mind . . . it was like being insulated from reality. The curtain was still down, and I knew that Annabelle and Charlotte were behind it, but for the time being they had simply ceased to exist, and all I could do was carry on with my ordinary life as though nothing had happened. I didn't say anything about them to Peter. The exhibition is still on, the gallery still full of visitors. We sat in his office and ate sandwiches and had a glass of beer, and watched them through the glass of the door as though they were goldfish in a tank. Those were my pictures they were looking at, but I couldn't relate myself either to the pictures or to them. Nothing seemed to have anything to do with me.

"Then I left Peter and I went out and started walking. It was a beautiful afternoon. I walked for miles along the embankment, and eventually I realized that I'd reached Millbank and I was standing outside the Tate Gallery. Do you know the Tate?"

"Yes."

"Do you go there?"

"Often."

"Do you know the Chantrey collection?"

"No."

"I went up the steps and into the gallery. I made for the room where the Chantrey collection is hung. There's a picture in it by John Singer Sargent. It's an oil. Quite big. Two little girls in a garden at night, lighting Japanese lanterns. They're wearing white dresses with frilled collars. There are lilies growing and pink roses. It's called *Carnation Lily, Lily Rose.* One of the little girls has short, dark hair and a very thin, delicate white neck, like the stem of a flower. She could be Charlotte.

"I don't know how long I stood there. But after a bit, very slowly, I realized that that safety curtain was going up, and little by little I was being flooded with—extraordinary instincts I'd never known I possessed. Tenderness. Protectiveness. Pride. And then anger. I began to be angry. Angry with all of them. Annabelle, and her husband and her mother. But most of all angry with myself. What the bloody hell was I doing, I asked myself, when she was my child, and I was her father, goddamn it. What the bloody hell was I doing, unloading all my responsibilities onto Phoebe? The answer was painfully simple. I was standing there doing nothing, which was what I had been doing for the past three days. Running on the spot, we used to call it at school. Getting nowhere. Achieving absolutely bugger all.

"I left the picture, and I went downstairs and found a telephone. I rang Directory enquiries and got Mrs. Tolliver's telephone number. And then I rang White Lodge. Mrs. Tolliver wasn't there . . ."

"She's visiting a friend in Helford," I told Daniel. I might just as well not have spoken.

". . . but her housekeeper answered the telephone and I told her that I was a friend of Leslie Collis and I wanted to get in touch with him, and

221

she was able to give me the name of the firm where he works in the City."

The kettle was boiling, but we both seemed to have forgotten about coffee. I switched it off and then went to pull out a chair and to sit at the other end of the table, so that Daniel and I faced each other down its long scrubbed length.

"So, another phone call. I rang Leslie Collis. I said I wanted to see him. He began by saying that it wasn't convenient, but I insisted it was urgent, so he finally said that he could give me fifteen minutes or so if I could come right away.

"I went out of the Tate and got a taxi and went to his office. The City was looking very beautiful. I'd forgotten how beautiful it is, with all those ponderous buildings and narrow streets, and everywhere sudden unexpected glimpses of St. Paul's. One day I must go back and do some drawings . . ."

The words died. He had lost the thread of what he was telling me.

"Leslie Collis," I reminded him gently.

"Yes, of course." He put up his hand and ran his fingers through his hair. He began to laugh. "It was the most ludicrous interview. In the first place, I was looking even more reprehensible than I usually do. Again, I don't think I'd shaved, and I was wearing the shirt I'd worn on the train, and a pair of sneakers with holes in the toes. He, on the other hand, was all resplendent in his City gear, starched collar, pinstripe suit. We made the most incongruous pair of antagonists. Anyway, I sat down and started to talk, and as soon as I mentioned Mrs. Tolliver and Charlotte, he immediately decided I'd come to blackmail him, and he was on his feet, shouting me down, threatening to call the police. And then I started shouting, too, just to try and make myself heard, and for a moment or two there was total pandemonium with both of us accusing each other, claiming responsibility, disclaiming responsibility, blaming each other, blaming Annabelle.

"But finally, just as I'd decided he was going to keel over with a heart attack and leave me with a corpse on my hands as well as everything else, it got through to him that I wasn't a villain come to bleed him white. After that things got a bit better. We both sat down again, and he lit a cigarette, and we started all over."

"You didn't *like* him, did you?"

"Why? Didn't you?"

"When I saw him that morning on the train, I thought he was the most horrible man."

"He's not that bad."

"But saying he never wants Charlotte again . . ."

"I know. That's rotten. But, in a way, I see his point of view. He's an ambitious man. He's worked his butt off all his life to make a lot of money and achieve his ambitions. I think he probably genuinely adored Annabelle. But he must have known all along, from the very first, that she could never be faithful to him. Even so, he stuck to her, gave her everything she wanted, bought the house in Sunningdale so that the boy could be brought up in the country. She had a car of her own, a maid, a gardener, holidays in Spain, total freedom. He kept saying, 'I gave her everything. I gave that woman bloody everything.'"

"Did he know from the first that Charlotte wasn't his baby?"

"Yes, of course he knew. He hadn't seen Annabelle for three months, and then she came back from Cornwall and told him that she was pregnant. And that's a pretty good kick in the balls for any self-respecting man."

"Why didn't he end it then?"

"He wanted to keep the family together. He's devoted to his son. He didn't want to lose face with his friends."

"He never liked Charlotte, though."

"It's hard to blame him for that."

"Did he say he didn't like her?"

"More or less. He said she was sly. He said she told lies."

"If she did, it was his fault."

"That's what I told him."

"That must have gone down well."

"Oh, it was all right. By then we'd reached the stage when all the cards were on the table, and we could insult each other as much as we liked, with no offence given or taken. It was almost as though we'd made friends."

It was hard to imagine. "But what did you *talk* about?"

"We talked about everything. I told him that Charlotte was going to stay with Phoebe, and in the end he finally admitted that he was grateful. And he was also quite pleased to hear that she wasn't going back to that school. Annabelle had chosen it for the child, but in his opinion it had never been worth the massive fees he'd had to fork out each term. I asked about the boy Michael, but Collis seemed to think that he was no problem. He's fifteen and apparently mature, well able to look after himself, do his own thing. I think the general feeling was that he'd outgrown his mother and, considering the way she was carrying on, would be better away from her influence. Leslie Collis is going to sell the house in the country and get a place in London. He and the boy will live there together."

"I'm sorry for Michael."

"I'm sorry for him, too. I'm sorry for everybody in this unholy mess. But I believe he'll probably be all right. The father thinks the world of him, and they appear to be the best of friends."

"And what about Annabelle?"

"He's spoken to his lawyer, and divorce proceedings are already underway. Leslie Collis is not a man to let the grass grow under his feet."

I waited for him to go on, but he didn't, so I said, "Which leaves us back at square one. What's going to happen to Charlotte? Or didn't you talk about her?"

"Of course we talked about her. That was the whole object of the exercise."

"Leslie Collis knows you're her father?"

"Sure, that was the first thing I told him. And he doesn't want her back."

"What about Annabelle? How does she feel about Charlotte?"

"She doesn't want her either, and even if she did, I don't think Leslie Collis would let her have the child. Call it sour grapes if you will, but it's the best thing that could happen to Charlotte."

"Why?"

"Because, my darling Prue, if Leslie Collis doesn't want Charlotte and neither does Annabelle, then the way is clear for me to adopt her as my own."

I sat still as stone, staring at him in incredulous disbelief.

"But they won't let you."

"Why not?"

"You're not married."

"The law has changed. Now a single person is allowed to adopt. It takes longer to get through the courts; there's obviously a bit more red tape to be cut, but it is eventually perfectly possible. Provided, of course, that Annabelle agrees to it, and I honestly don't see why she shouldn't."

"But you haven't got a house. You haven't got anywhere to live."

"Yes I have. Lewis Falcon is off to the south of France to work there for a couple of years, and he said he'd rent me his house at Lanyon and the studio if I wanted them. So I'll be around. I don't suppose I'd be able to have Charlotte to live with me until the adoption is through the courts, but

I'm hoping that Phoebe might be able to continue as her official foster mother until then."

"It sounds . . . Oh, Daniel, it sounds too good to be true."

"I know. And as I said, the extraordinary thing was that by the end of all this, it was almost as though Leslie Collis and I had made friends. We seemed to understand each other. Finally we went out to lunch together, to a scruffy place where none of his colleagues would spy him with a down-and-out like me. And at the end of the meal, there was another ludicrous pantomime while we both tried to pick up the bill. Neither of us wanted to owe the other anything. So in the end we split it down the middle and each paid half. And then we went out of the restaurant, and we said good-bye, and I promised to be in touch. And he walked back to his office, and I got into a taxi and went back to the gallery to see Peter Chastal.

"I knew I had to get a good lawyer, and I've never even had a bad one, because Peter's always done everything for me. I've never even had an accountant, either, or a banker, or an agent. Peter's handled everything ever since that first day when I went to him, raw and inexperienced, sent by Chips. He was marvellous. He put me in touch with his own lawyer, and he went and found out how much money I had put away, which is about ten times more than I thought I had, and then he said it was about time I matched up to this new family-man image and got over my dread of anything mechanical and bought myself a car. So I went out and did. And then Peter and I had dinner together, and after that I knew I couldn't wait another moment to see you all, so I got into the car and drove back to Cornwall."

"And now Phoebe and Charlotte aren't even *here*." I couldn't bear it for him.

But he only said, "I'm glad they're not. Because the most important thing I've got to tell you concerns you. Actually, it's not so much telling you as asking you. I'm going to Greece. For a holiday. In about ten days' time. I've told you about the house on Spetsai, and I've already asked you to come with me, but now I'm asking you again. I've got two seats booked on a flight to Athens. If Lily and Phoebe can cope with Charlotte, will you come with me?" The sugar-cube house that I had told myself I would never see. The whitewashed terrace with the geraniums, and the boat with a sail like the wing of a gull. "Come with me, Prue."

My mind raced ahead. I would have to do things, arrange things, tell people. My mother.

Marcus Bernstein. And, somehow I should have to write a letter to poor Nigel Gordon.

I said, "Yes."

Down the length of the table our eyes met and held. He suddenly smiled. He said, "How little we know each other. Was it you who said that, or I?"

"It was you."

"After two weeks in Greece we'll know each other so much better."

"Yes. I expect we will."

"And after that—after we get home—perhaps we could think about coming back to Lanyon together. We'd have to get married first, but we don't need to think about that just now. It's better that way. After all, we don't either of us want to commit ourselves, do we?"

I knew that there was nothing I wanted more. And from the way Daniel was looking at me, I had a pretty good idea that he felt the same way.

I smiled, too. "No," I told him. "We don't want to commit ourselves."

When Mr. Thomas's taxi returned bearing Phoebe and Charlotte and all their shopping, we were still in the kitchen, though no longer sitting at either end of the table. We heard the ancient vehicle come grinding down the road and turn in at the gate, and we went out together to greet them.

Mr. Thomas was flummoxed by Daniel's car, which, unexpectedly parked in front of the house, had left him no room to turn. Phoebe was already out of the taxi, dramatic in her best brown tweed cape, and trying to give him directions.

"Left hand down, Mr. Thomas. No, I don't mean left, I mean right . . ."

"Phoebe," said Daniel.

She turned and saw him.

"Daniel!"

Mr. Thomas and his problems were forgotten. Disgusted, he switched off his engine and sat there, brooding, trapped, the radiator of his car nose-to-nose with Daniel's, the back wheels hard against the red brick kerbstone that protected Phoebe's border.

Daniel moved to meet her halfway. They embraced enormously, and her hat was knocked sideways.

"You wicked villain." She thumped his shoulder lovingly with her good fist. "Where have you been?"

But she did not give him time to tell her, because just then, over his shoulder, she caught sight of me standing there in Lily's apron and with a smile on my face that I could do nothing about. She let go of Daniel and came to me, and although she had no idea of what had happened, what was happening, what was going to happen, I saw my own happiness reflected in her face, and we held each other very tightly and laughed together, because Daniel had come back, and everything was suddenly so completely all right.

And Charlotte. At the same instant we remembered Charlotte. We looked and saw her cautiously alighting from the back of the old car, her arms filled with a perilous pile of wrapped boxes and packages. I knew that she had watched us all, was holding back, probably telling herself that she, Charlotte, had no place in all these loving reunions. Carefully, with her foot, she closed the door of the taxi. When she turned, her chin clamped over the topmost parcel, she found herself confronted by Daniel. Slowly her face tilted up to stare into his, her eyes unblinking behind the owlish spectacles. For a moment there was silence as they looked at each other. And then Daniel smiled and said, "Hello, my love. I'm back again."

He held wide his arms. It was all she needed. "Oh, Daniel . . ."

The parcels began to slip. She let them go and flung herself at him, and he caught her and swung her up in his arms, round and round, and the packages lay unheeded where they had tumbled, higgledy-piggledy onto the gravel.

ROSAMUNDE PILCHER

THE SHELL SEEKERS

At the end of a long and useful life, Penelope Keeling's prize possession is *The Shell Seekers*, painted by her father, and symbolizing her unconventional life, from bohemian childhood to wartime romance. When her grown children learn their grandfather's work is now worth a fortune, each has an idea as to what Penelope should do. But as she recalls the passions, tragedies, and secrets of her life, she knows there is only one answer . . . and it lies in her heart.

AVAILABLE WHEREVER BOOKS ARE SOLD FROM ST. MARTIN'S PAPERBACKS

SS 01/01

ROSAMUNDE PILCHER

COMING HOME

In 1935, Judith Dunbar is left behind at a British boarding school when her mother and baby sister go off to join her father in Singapore. At Saint Ursula's, her friendship with Loveday Carey-Lewis sweeps her into the privileged, madcap world of the British aristocracy, teaching her about values, friendship, and wealth. But it will be the drama of war, as it wrenches Judith from those she cares about most, that will teach her about courage . . . and about love.

"Rosamunde Pilcher's most satisfying story since *The Shell Seekers*." —*Chicago Tribune*

"Captivating . . . The best sort of book to come home to . . . Readers will undoubtedly hope Pilcher comes home to the typewriter again soon." —*New York Daily News*